Antonija Mežnarić

The Lost Treasure Hunters and Other Tales of Folk Terrors

Antonija Mežnarić

The Lost Treasure Hunters and Other Tales of Folk Terrors

ISBN

ebook 978-953-8360-27-5

paperback 978-953-8360-28-2

Edited by

Vesna Kurilić

Cover and interior art by

Antonio Filipović

Rijeka, 2024

shtriga.com

shtrigabooks@gmail.com

Antonija Mežnarić

THE LOST TREASURE HUNTERS

AND

OTHER TALES OF FOLK TERRORS

Rijeka, 2024

Content Warnings

The Mystery of the Lost "Treasure Hunters of Velebit": Overview of the Material

This novella contains disturbing imagery depicting body horror and gore, animal cruelty, implied rape, and implied dubious consent.

To Stop the Screaming

Warnings for implied (off-screen) rape, implied (off-screen) spousal abuse, religious trauma, rape culture and victim blaming, mentions of intrusive thoughts, mentions of self-harm ideation and suicidal ideation, mentions of forced pregnancy, graphic depiction of gore and child harm, and mentions of animal cruelty.

Table of Content

The Lost Treasure Hunters

The Mystery of the Lost "Treasure Hunters of Velebit": Overview of the Material

edited by Karla Beg

Preface

AT THE MOMENT OF my writing this preface, I believe that everybody is already familiar with the famous case of the lost "Velebit treasure hunters", as it was coined by the trite, sensationalist media known for easy copy-pasting. The disappearance of the five people on the Velebit mountain wasn't originally hot news for the journalists in the time of year that's well-known for tourists experiencing a myriad of accidents on our hiking trails. After a few articles, reports, and posts on social media, this event was soon overshadowed by the brutal death of a diver run over by a speedboat by the island of Hvar. The media circus over the "treasure hunters" only started after a single person of the missing five was finally found a few weeks after the disappearance—dehydrated, disoriented, verbally incoherent, and with severe physical injuries—in the early morning hours, somewhere close to the trail leading to the Alan mountain hut. The re-emergence of Hrvoje Beg was the first domino to fall, which would, in a short time, result with various theories, some from the officials, some from the true crime fanatics on socials, all thanks to some police information leaking to the public, and the fact that Hrvoje still can't, to this day—almost a year after the event—explain what had exactly happened to him.

Today, this case should've been old news, still intriguing only to the most hard-core conspiracy theorist, but, deeply unfortunate, the podcast *The Cursed Expedition of Velebit's Hidden Gold*—hosted by the popular true crime podcasters Vesna Hani-Kriletić, Igor Morinić, and Tonija Zvončarić—reinvigorated the general public's interest in the mystery. At this time, the podcast is nearing its final episode, which will, knowing this particular trio, surely be dramatic. Not to mention how, with each new episode, they're reopening wounds that had never fully healed in the first place.

If you ask me, I have no idea how this podcast got so popular. All of the information they had was already well-known—chewed up, ingested, and vomited out in perpetuum—and while Hrvoje is lost in his own mind, potential new findings are going to stay undiscovered. Still, that's not deterring the clout-chasing bastards trying to dig through his trauma to find answers. Which brings us to my reason for collecting this material and publishing it this way.

A quick eye has probably caught the tidbit that Hrvoje and I share a surname. It's not a secret that he's my younger brother, which is why I've also had a lot of problems with tiresome journalists, nosy youtubers, and true crime vultures. You may have heard that I've refused all interview invites, including a guest spot for the aforementioned podcast. Simply said, the whole situation was nauseating, and I was acutely aware of the ghoulish exploitation of my family's tragedy for profit. Neither Hrvoje, nor our parents, nor his partner Saša, nor I, are clowns dancing for public amusement. What my family needed, desperately, was some peace and quiet, so my little brother could recover, without constant surveillance and analysis of his every movement, no matter how unimportant and small. We couldn't get that one thing. And, recently, with this renewed interest in the case thanks to the podcast, *some* amateur investigators crossed the line. They managed to bribe the medical staff of the psychiatric hospital in Lopača to get Hrvoje alone for an interview, which, of course, ended catastrophically. That's the source of that infamous video that circulated all over the Internet before we managed to get it removed. (But everyone knows that what gets posted once on the net is never truly gone, and I know for a fact that too many people downloaded the video before it was taken care of.) As if the psychotic episode of a heavily traumatized person is entertainment. Truthfully, the only reason why I write this Preface in the safety of my home, and not a prison cell, is because my brother needs caregivers, not avengers, but oh my, I've wanted to run *somebody* over with my car so much, that's for sure.

(I don't care that my threats will become public once I publish this, bless selfpub, where I can do whatever I want, and if you are reading this, you can be ashamed, I hope you won't get a second of peace in your miserable life, always looking over your shoulder, never sure if there's somebody lurking in the shadows.)

So, you could say that I have a personal stake in this case. From that first unsettling moment when my phone call to Hrvoje went unanswered for the fifth time, to the vertigo when I heard from Saša that his calls aren't getting through either, culminating in the moment of dissociation when we first spoke to Croatian Mountain Rescue Service (HGSS), learning that my brother had gotten lost. From all the sleepless nights I've spent crying, imagining Hrvoje lying somewhere on the rocks, broken and dead. Even though I'm eternally grateful to all the gods and creatures that can hear me for his return, I find myself in a constant state of worry about what lies on the other side of his mind's locked door. I want to know, as is normal, what happened. Not only to settle my nerves, but also to be able to give him better support and help to heal and move on.

Besides, I'm still in contact with the families of the rest of his missing group and I'm deeply empathizing with their pain over the lack of information. For them, the suffering didn't stop, didn't get reduced with Hrvoje's resurfacing. I can only hope that one day we'll have all the answers, that Hrvoje will be better enough to tell us the truth, even though they're all pretty sure, at this point, that their loved ones are long dead. I know that, if nothing else is possible, they would like to find the bodies for burial, to get some closure.

Considered as missing, presumably dead, are: Lorena Matić, her wife Marina Kružić—the two were the organizers of the whole trip—their mountain guide Slobodan Relić, and Silva Horvat, the folklorist. I feel an obligation to write a few words about them, so it'll be easier for you to follow the material in the case you have lived in a cave this last year or if you're reading this booklet somewhere down the line in the future, when, hopefully, this case isn't in constant public spotlight.

Lorena and Marina are popular youtubers with the channel *Hidden Croatia*, dedicated to touristy vlogs with a focus on local folk tales, myths, and urban legends of the places they visited. They used to frequent small Croatian villages and municipalities, towns and cities, both isolated places and popular tourist destinations, then publish their video travelogues in which they showcased the location and its stories. They used to have medium-level popularity on YouTube with some 250k followers (in the meantime, the number has jumped to one million). They filmed in Croatian with subtitles in English, German, Italian, and Spanish, which is the reason for their popularity among tourists and Croatians alike. Often, they got brand deals and sponsorships from tourist agencies of the places they visited. Lorena majored in Cultural Studies at the Faculty of Humanities and Social Sciences in Rijeka, and she was also a registered tourist guide, with a talent for travel vlogs. On the other hand, Marina was the one who dealt with their social media presence, PR, and video editing, while her day job was a position at a marketing firm I'm not going to name here, since it's irrelevant.

Silva Horvat is their close friend, and this was the first time that she joined in on their travel. She worked at the Institute for Ethnology and Folklore in Zagreb, and the main reason she decided to join was her work on a paper about oral traditions of Northern Velebit. Her husband was born and raised in one of the small towns in the foothills of Velebit, and he explained how Silva wanted to collect stories from the elders that still live in the more isolated, harder to reach villages from that region, and publish them in her paper.

Slobodan Relić, originally from the town of Karlobag, was hired as a mountain guide for the group. The tough fifty-year-old was an experienced hiker and a Velebit expert, and as a member of a hiking club, he was used to leading hikers and tourist groups on multi-day trips all over the mountain, telling them local stories. Silva's husband was the one who recommended Slobodan.

The fifth member of this group was, of course, Hrvoje. My brother knows Lorena and Marina from their college days, and he used to occasionally help them with their videos. For him, this trip was supposed to be, more or less, a vacation, lending a hand with equipment included (though we can see on the video recordings that he took over the role of cameraman, probably of his own accord). He was also on a quest for inspiration for his podcast about ghosts and cursed Croatian locations, which had a smaller, but very enthusiastic audience. Of course, the podcast's popularity exploded with his return, and is now astronomical. I hate that it wasn't his hard work and creativity that made him so popular instead of a tragedy, but that is, I guess, human nature for you.

There are multiple theories about what could've happened to the group. Lorena and Marina never talked about the nature of their relationship in videos and they could easily pass for friends sharing an interest, but once the case became a media sensation, the truth was brought out into the open. Since they were a lesbian couple, along with the fact that my brother was loudly out and proud on his socials, resulted in the most popular speculation—supported by police officials—that the group suffered a hate crime by some unidentified locals. With Slobodan and Silva as accidental victims. That theory is supported by my brother's documented injuries, consistent with the signs of a brutal physical attack as well as bites from a large dog. Hrvoje, though, vehemently refuses that version of events, but is unable to verbalize what actually happened. The police believe that Hrvoje had managed to run away from his attackers, and *survive* several weeks lost and alone on a *mountain*, without any food or water sources, while the rest of them are lying somewhere in a shallow grave or at the bottom of a slope. I don't think I need to explain to you that I believe my brother, wholeheartedly.

On the other hand, the camera (damaged), Hrvoje's mobile phone, Lorena's dream journal (half soaked through and bloody), found on Hrvoje, tell another tale. The more fantastical one, spawning theories about fairies and werewolves. Of course, it's way more probable that all of the written notes were a result of hallucinations created by a dehydrated brain, rather than proof of something supernatural happening on the mountain. You can clearly see how both Hrvoje and Lorena became unhinged with time, which is completely understandable in their situation. People hiking on the mountain during the summer without plenty of water can easily and swiftly get lost in mental delusions. Just because they wrote it down, doesn't make it real. But Hrvoje's psychosis doesn't help eliminate these kinds of theories, especially not after that short video showing him trying to peel his own skin off with his nails, believing that he's a werewolf imprisoned in the body of a human. *Oh, how I hate that video.*

The easiest of all the conclusions is that they simply got lost. Slobodan was already older, maybe he suffered a sunstroke, and in his condition, wandered off the trail, the group in tow. Then they perished of natural causes—either falling down the slopes, snake bites, or from dehydration. Velebit is full of nooks and crannies, wild trees and underbrush, where their bodies could be hidden from the rescue searchers' view. That, of course, doesn't explain Hrvoje's injuries. Except that he may have run into a wolf—which isn't impossible, there are wolves on Northern Velebit, it's just that it's rare for people to encounter them on the trails. But if he was alone, and quiet enough, he could have ended up finding a she-wolf with her litter, which would be dangerous in any situation, but especially in his condition. Or he encountered a hungry lone wolf, which saw in him the potential for a meal. I'm only glad that, whatever happened, Hrvoje was the one who got out of that encounter alive.

The booklet you currently have in your hands is the result of Saša's and my investigation. Some of the things here will be familiar to you from before because they were leaked, like some of the recordings or Hrvoje's notes, but some will be completely new information, published for the first time. The collected material consists of emails, journal entries, Viber and text messages, and transcripts of all the video footage. I won't publish the raw video recordings until I have all the necessary permissions. I've tried to arrange these materials into a coherent narrative to the best of my ability. A lot of it was thrown out simply because it was unimportant; for example, I didn't include the first recorded video in which Lorena and Marina are presenting the rest of the Velebit team to their future viewers, because I already wrote down all the information relevant to the case, so it would've been redundant. Besides, photos posted on their socials before they disappeared, the YouTube channel, and Hrvoje's podcast, are all available for your perusal if you wish. This booklet is simply my attempt to give voice to the people who aren't here to say what happened to them, and the one person who isn't of sound mind to do that.

The map I'm attaching at the beginning is a product of Saša's and my hard work researching possible points where the group could've walked off the path, since we didn't get anything sensible from the police. I didn't edit any of the written records of the group, not even to proofread mistakes and fix typos; I've just added context for each at the beginning, so it makes for an easier reading experience. I even added all of the links as they were used in the emails, so you can click on them and check them out yourself (of course, if you read this in print, no clicking for you, but you can google the names and see for yourself). I'm publishing all of this in the hope that full transparency will erase the constant barrage on my brother, who, in any case, wouldn't tell you anything different from what is collected here.

Read this, come to your own conclusions over what had happened, believe in whatever you want to believe, and leave my family, and the family of the missing ones, alone. All of the information you need and want is here. There will be no new info from us because this is all we have.

Here you go, I give you absolutely everything, so now fuck off.

May 2nd, 2025
Karla Beg

THE COLLECTED MATERIAL

1. A scan of my hastily drawn sketch of the Northern Velebit National Park area (only the pertinent section). I've been informed by my legal help that I can't just attach a scan of the map Saša and I used to orient ourselves while searching for clues. Instead, here's my drawing. If you want the real thing, you should get yourself the map by Zlatko Smerke, published by SMAND. I know that plenty of amateur investigators fooled around with Google maps, however, in this case, Google is completely useless. You need to use a professional hiking map.

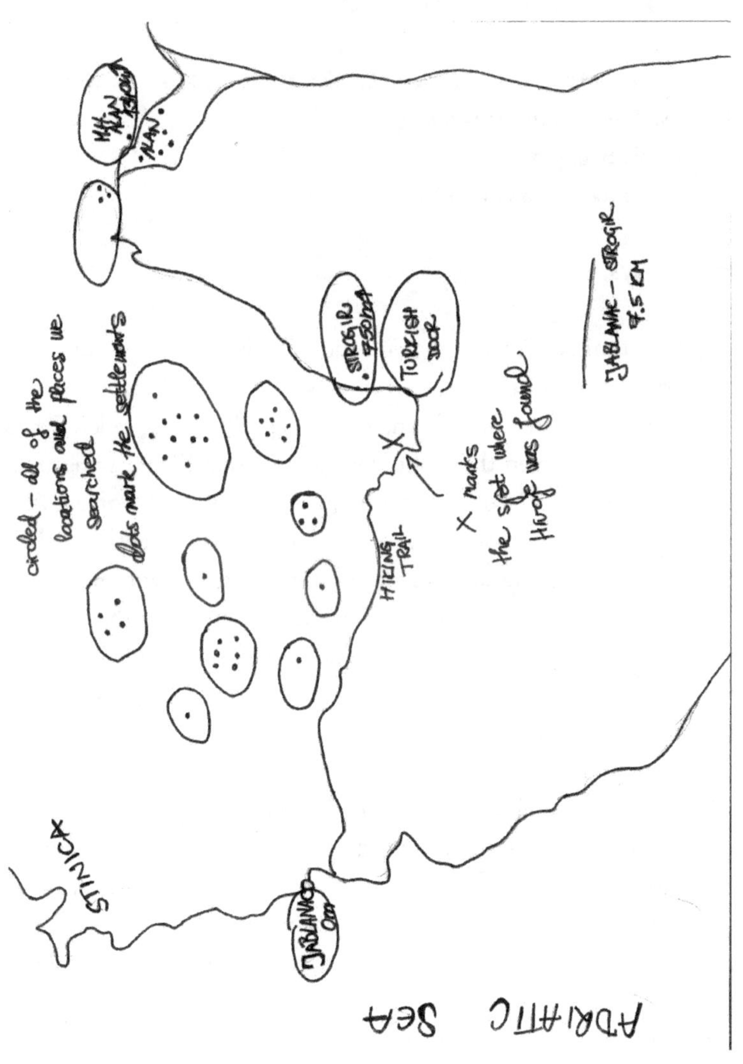
circled - all of the locations and places we searched
dots mark the settlements
HIKING TRAIL
TURKISH DOOR
STINICA
ADRIATIC SEA

2. Email correspondence between Lorena, Silva, and Hrvoje, about the original idea, plans, and attachments (I've accessed the emails from Hrvoje's account)

From: Lorena Matić <lori.dreamer@skrovitahrvatska.hr> 24. 04. 2024. 17:45
To: Silva Horvat (hotmail.com)
Cc: Hrvoje Beg (gmail.com)
Subject: an idea for a new video

Hello, guys,

As promised, I'm sending you the folktale that I wrote down to the best of my memory. Silva, I'm so sorry that my recollection is spotty and for forgetting the name of the teller haha teller! I had been a brooding teen then who had no idea that I'll be a youtuber one day, nor did I know what a teller is, and the old woman who told me the story was only a regular ancient Croatian baba™ Problem is, we had vacationed a few summers in a row in the Stinica camp, so my best guess is that I heard the tale either in the summer of 2003, 2004, or 2005. I have no idea how to find the baba since I forgot her name, and since she had been as old as Methuselah when I was a teen, I'm going to assume that she's not with us anymore.

I think that she was from Jablanac, but when I try hard to remember the details, my memory becomes fuzzy and all mixed up, just like with the correct wording of the story—I'm absolutely certain that, that summer, we went from the camp to Jablanac town for ice cream and pizza. I'm certain that, when I talked with the old woman, it was in front of her house—you know very well how our elders sometimes sit in front of their open doors in summer—but in my head, the image is a bit different. In my memory, there's one vision of the baba standing upright, not hunched over, as is the usual case, carrying a cane from some sort of stunted wood in her wrinkled but strong hands, with a headscarf so green that it was competing with the greenery of the nature around us, because we were in the forest, near the camp. I remember the incessant chirping of crickets sawing my brain, and the smell of salt in the air. But that doesn't make any sense, because, what would a baba do in the midst of the forest, all alone? And I'm 100% sure we were alone. Anyway, that's just the short impression left in my brain, probably copied over from some other memory and superimposed over the real one, because I'm also sure I talked with her in Jablanac, where the old woman was draped over her cane, hunched down by the weight of the years sitting on her shoulders. And she didn't wear a green headscarf, but black, just like the rest of the clothing was black.

I'm certain that, when she told the story, it was in some sort of dialect or local idiom, but I have no idea how to retell it authentically, so this is my best reconstruction.

And, in the end, you'll probably find this funny, but sometimes I see her in my dreams, the one with the green headscarf, and in my dreams, she opens her mouth, except, it wasn't a mouth but jaws filled with sharp canines, and I'm screaming my throat raw, running back to the camp, but the camp is empty and desolate, and in the sea I can see corpses floating, bloated from water and salt, and among them are my mother and sister, completely green and swelled in their faces, and then I wake up drenched in sweat, on my pillow soaked in tears, and in that few moments before my mind catches up, I'm completely sure they're dead, that they have been dead all this time.

I'm mulling over whether I should also tell my dream in the video or not. I mean, the creepy dream is great, no? It will spice up the whole story, and you know how people love spooky shit. But on the other hand, the dream is a bit too personal, you know? What do you think?

Anyway, I'm rambling. Silva, there's a chance your husband might recognize the folk tale. I already have some plans on how we could organize the trip, but I'm sure you'll have a much better idea! Marina is fine with anything, she just wants to hike, take bunch of photos, and swim hahaha

Hrvoje, what are the chances of Saša getting a vacay so he can also join us? I'm going to guess none, but you can always hope. He also deserves to take some time off.

This is so exciting! I'm so so happy.

Talk to you soon,

Lori

Email attachment—the folktale Lorena had heard on a summer vacation when she was a teen

[I don't remember the correct beginning of the tale, was it "once upon a time"? but no, I think not, in my memory it starts like this, I will put down anything I'm not 100% certain about in square brackets]

The Turks came here, where we stand now, but the mountain didn't love them. The rocks didn't want them. The stones didn't want them. Nor did the trees nor did the grass [nor the well nor the snakes]. But wherever the Turks went the blood followed. And the blood was [sweet? strong?]. Cutting down, spilling the blood, hiding, ravaging the land, they stumbled upon a door. On the other side there was gold [treasure? but no, I think it was gold because of the rest of the tale], so shiny that it beamed like a torch seen all the way to the other mountain top, that the night became the day because it shone brightly like the sun in the sky. And the Turks crossed over for the gold, their eyes overshadowed by lust [greed?]. They didn't come back. The mountain was happy. [And satiated. Finally fed and watered.]

The gold is still there, on the top, behind the doors, bright as a star, voracious like wildfire. It waits and waits for someone to finally find it and hold it in their hands. [Do you want to see the treasure? I can show it to you, just come with me. Come, girl, come. Don't tell me you're afraid of the old, feeble granny.]

From: Hrvoje Beg <beg.hr90@gmail.com> 24. 04. 2024. 18:17
To: Lorena Matić (skrovitahrvatska.hr)
Cc: Silva Horvat (hotmail.com)
Re: Subject: the idea for new video

fuck me, Lori, I got chills. all right, all right, I see you're planning to steer into no sleep reddit vibes. croatian folklore but like a horrorish urban legend has so much potential. you have my support for both the dream and this gimmick with the luring baba. the follower count will grow like shrooms.

and to answer your question—no, saša can't come with us, the supermarket would topple down like a tower of babel if they were to give him vacation time in june. you know how it goes. hashtag exploitation. but he's cool with me going, and he says hi!

B

From: Lorena Matić <lori.dreamer@skrovitahrvatska.hr> 24. 04. 2024. 18:45
To: Hrvoje Beg (gmail.com)
Cc: Silva Horvat (hotmail.com)
Re: Re: Subject: the idea for new video

Hrvoje, I'm not sure what exactly prompted your reply, the story isn't any bloodier than the rest of our folk tales. :D But I agree with you that Croatian folk horror is a bit underused, especially in tourism. I know that there were some tours like that, I heard about that ghost tour happening in Veprinac in Opatija, with štrigas, moras, and werewolves, which, if you ask me, is such a great idea for catching the tourists' eye! But I wasn't planning on horror vibes, my current video idea is more in the style of hunting for a hidden treasure, which I believe no one has tried to use before! Like, National Treasure, just without the kidnapping of the Croatian president.

I'm guessing that Silva is still writing a dissertation for the reply haha I'm giddy with excitement to see what she has for us!

Lori

From: Silva Horvat <silva.horvat85@hotmail.com> 24. 04. 2024. 20:23
To: Lorena Matić (skrovitahrvatska.hr)
Cc: Hrvoje Beg (gmail.com)
Re: Re: Re: Subject: the idea for new video

Dear Lori and Hrvoje,

here's my reply, which, no, Lori, it's not an academic paper. :)

I read your folk tale to Roko, but he's never heard of it. The story that his grandma used to tell him was about the lost ninth Roman well. For those who don't know—according to the stories, Velebit has eight Roman wells, and a ninth that is lost to us, but in which the hidden Roman treasure lies, and the only way to find this ninth well is to locate it in your dreams. It's guarded by a snake, and in some versions of the tale, you can find an imprisoned maiden with the treasure, and sometimes you need to kiss the snake to release the girl.

Now, your tale isn't so unusual on its own. It has more than a few common elements of the oral folklore of the Velebit foothills: first the obvious—the hidden Velebit treasure; in some stories, the treasure was originally from the Ottoman conquerors, sometimes, it's the gold of the king Bela, or it's a hajduk treasure, or even fairy treasure, and sometimes, as mentioned, it's from the Romans.

The Turkish people are another common motif in these tales and it's not unusual for the story to be so bloody—obviously, because of the Ottoman invasion; I believe I don't need to explain why it was that they were the go-to villain in old stories—for example, there's a tale that the village called *Lomivrat* got its name because it's the place where Ottomans literally *broke their necks* when they fell down the gorge, and that to this day, you can see their floating corpses where they landed in the Adriatic sea (I think you can connect this trivia to your own dream, if you wish to use this parallel for the video). Snakes are also a very common story motif, so it's a good chance that the teller mentioned them, especially if she mentioned wells, so there's a possibility it was a reference to this other tale of hidden Velebit treasure (I say this because of what you wrote in one of the square brackets).

It's in my opinion that the folk tale you heard is actually a version of the story about the hidden treasure up on Strogir. Strogir (pic here) is a mountain monolit above Jablanac town, very popular with alpinists, near the pass called the Turkish Door (another pic!) which I believe is what the teller meant when she said that the Turks [...] *stumbled upon a door.* One of the stories about the hidden Velebit treasure mentions the gold brightly lighting up the hilltop during the night, which is seen by a married couple in the tale. It is an old belief that the treasure is hidden at the top of Strogir, so that whoever manages to climb to the top will get rich. And how did it get there? Well, the tellers will say that this particular treasure was left by the fae folk, though, you'll have them *truthfully* disclosing that they can't say for sure it's the truth, but that it's what *the stories tells us* (as is common for our tellers, to sound more credible during storytelling).

There's a great academic paper about the oral traditions of the Velebit foothills, short and easy to read, with the collected folk tales I mentioned here, by the author Matija Dronjić, who explains that the reason for the popularity of the hidden treasure stories on Velebit is that the people living on it were extremely poor. You can download the paper at this link, it's really an amazing source!

So it's not that surprising that the inhabitants of the Velebit villages had multiple versions of these stories where some lucky person finds a treasure and becomes instantly rich. That's why I believe that your folk tale is just another variant, as of yet uncollected, but with your permission, I would like to record it.

Of course, it's a bit tricky that you have very few details about the teller.

And, of course, I would record the tale without the last square bracket. But, if you wish, you can definitely use it to intrigue your watchers. Here I agree with Hrvoje's assessment.

Now, Lori, I know that you're the one planning the trip, but if you really want to spin the video as a "hunt for hidden treasure", I suggest that we start with Strogir, and then continue on to Karlobag town, and then we can again hike back up the mountain from there, following these diverse stories. The first rute would then be: Jablanac—Turkish Door—Strogir—mountain hut Alan. With superficial googling, I found a hiking path we can use. Since none of us are experienced hikers, I would like for us to have a mountain guide. If it's okay with you, I would like to ask Roko for help with that, if he has someone to recommend for this region.

Best,
Silva

From: Lorena Matić <lori.dreamer@skrovitahrvatska.hr> 24. 04. 2024. 22:02
To: Silva Horvat (hotmail.com)
Cc: Hrvoje Beg (gmail.com)
Re: Re: Re: Re: Subject: the idea for new video

... I don't know how to tell you this without sounding completely bonkers haha but, after your last two emails, I went back to read my folk tale. And I really, honestly, I promise you that, don't remember writing down the last square bracket. It must be something I dragged out from my subconsciousness while forcing myself to remember the tale the closest to how the baba™ told it. But otherwise I don't remember that part. Or writing it. How weird. Honestly, I'm a bit sleep deprived, it's probably because of that. No matter, I agree with you that this is a great concept for the video, so I think I'm going to use it! Just think about it, my stupid teen self could've disappeared because she was talking with a strange old woman in the middle of the forest. That's a spin! We could use new brand deals, especially because Marina's job is currently... on shaky legs, to say the least.

Anyway, Silva, thank you sooooo much for this paper, I agree that it's an amazing source! And I totally agree with everything you said! I would also like to start with Strogir, just, if there was a treasure there on the top, it must've been already picked up by some alpinist. :D

When you find the mountain guide, drop us his contact info so Marina can call him and arrange the details.

I'm so excited I could jump out of my own skin!

Bye, bye
Lori

3. An excerpt from the messages exchanged between Marina and Hrvoje, at the time while the group were working out trip details over email.

Marina
I'm not sure what to do anymore, tbh.
20:38

Did you see that story?
20:38

She really claims she doesn't remember writing down those creepy last sentences.
20:39

...
20:39

sorry, I thought she was fucking with us
20:39

Marina
I wish! What I wouldn't give for that to be true. But no. She's been struggling with night terrors for some time. Terrors! First, there had been nightmares in college, but they weren't so frequent. But
now it has transformed into night terrors paralyzing her with such a strong fear that I need to calm
her down. And now this... and she refuses to go to therapy, to ask for help, nothing. She's sleeping
less and less... I'm losing my mind here. And she's the one fooling around. Joking that it's the mora haunting her dreams. Mora! As in the nightmare creature from folk tales.
20:41

fuck, I'm so sorry...
20:41

Marina
I think she has some kind of anxiety problem. So all of it gets dredged up while she sleeps. But I can't help her since she doesn't want help. I can only hope that whatever issues she's struggling with she'll find a way to relax and chill out with this trip. It's always better when we're traveling and filming a new video.

20:42

I really don't need this shit right now. My boss is screwing with my brain. More and more colleagues are getting sacked... I think they want to get rid of me too. And this job is the only thing keeping us financially secure. Lori refuses to be a tourist guide, she doesn't want to do anything except youtube, and you know yourself how uncertain that source of revenue is. I'm also struggling with anxiety. I'm constantly on the edge. But I can't have a breakdown. I don't have that privilege. Not now.

20:44

you know I'm here for you two, you don't need to go through this shit alone. have a breakdown with me if you need to. Saša and I are here to help with the pieces

20:45

whatever you need, we're here to help
20:45

Marina
Thank you, so much. <3 Right now, this treasure hunt is helping. We'll see what to do after.
20:45

if you need me, I can run your boss over
20:46

saša will help me hide the body
20:46

nbd
20:47

we've listened to enough true crime podcasts that we know how to do this without leaving a trace ;)
20:47

Marina
Hahahahahahahahahah
20:48

You're such a fucking fool, but you're our fool
20:48

(your offer is very, very tempting, I admit)

20:49

4. Transcript of the video footage filmed in Jablanac town on July 21st, 2024, the night before the group started their hike for Strogir. It was filmed at dusk, the golden hues bathing the image, while in the background, you can glimpse a yellow tone dominating the horizon, like an egg yolk spilling over the sky. Depending on the angle of the shot, what's visible is either the calm blue sea or the stone facade of the rented apartment, where the group filmed on the terrace.

The video shows Lorena, Silva, and Marina, in that order of appearance, while Hrvoje's commentary can only be heard in audio. Lorena is a pale woman with short blonde hair falling to her shoulders, so translucently white you could mistake her for a German or Scandinavian tourist. Her cheeks, forehead, and neck have the unmistakable reddish traces of the sun, and her skin is glistening from a greasy sunscreen. Silva is a tanned woman sitting at the table by her side, with long, lush, curly black hair lightly peppered with gray. Marina is occasionally visible in the background, sitting in the beach chair with the laptop in her lap, and when she does show up in the shot, she's mostly checking her phone, with photosensitive lenses on her eyeglasses and sporting a short hairdo—the so called sidecut—in the unnatural dark shade of rust or dry blood.

Two wine glasses are visible on the table, filled with white wine, and an almost empty jug. Marina has a glass with clear liquid, probably water, filled with ice. The glass is on the floor by her feet, and at times you can see her drinking from it.

Hrvoje [in the background]: Aaaaand, we're filming.

Lorena [with a wide smile]: Jablanac is beautiful. A small coastal town, with the mountain like a crown upon its head. It touches both the sky and the depths of the earth. [she bursts into laughter] Okay, this is bad, we'll probably have to cut it out.

[Hrvoje is laughing in the background. Silva is also smiling, flipping her hair above her left shoulder.]

Lorena [continuing]: We're currently enjoying ourselves on the terrace of our rental, looking at the twilight and drinking local wine, brought to us by our dear mountain guide, whom you still didn't get a chance to meet, but you will, soon. [Lorena toasts to the camera and takes a sip, and then the camera turns and catches their surroundings, showing us the view of the sea covered in boats of different sizes and types lazily rocking on the surface. Then the image turns back to the table, with a focus on Lorena.] Don't worry, I filmed plenty of B roll to show you this quaint town from every possible angle, all of its colorful houses, coffee shops, restaurants, beaches. And, as usual, in the description you'll find all the useful links, like the one bringing you to the site where you can get yourself this sweet white wine. But let's go to the important part. [Lorena leans conspiratorially over the camera and claps her hands.] Tomorrow's plans! We have an exciting day before us, starting from dawn. Silva! [She turns toward the other woman at the table and the camera follows her, focusing on Silva, who, for a short moment, appears like a deer in the headlights. With her dark, wide open eyes, and lips pursed in a slight smile it seems like she wants to apologize for something.] Tell us, what to expect?

Silva [with a slight smile]: Early wake-up call at five o'clock, so we can begin our hike before the sun starts scorching the land.

Hrvoje [in the background]: Fucking torture, if you ask me. [Laughter from everyone at the table. In the background, the camera catches Marina. She's the only one who doesn't join in the laughter, instead, she's frowning, her eyes glued to the laptop.]

Lorena [dramatically pointing at her own face]: But an early start is extremely necessary, as you can see from my experience.

I burn too easily, despite me constantly smearing SPF 50 all over my skin. If it continues like this, I'll end up looking like a red bull's horn pepper.

Hrvoje [in the background]: Good thing that you don't have a brand deal with Daylong, otherwise this wouldn't look great for them.

Silva [ignoring Hrvoje, while Lorena is trying to stifle her laughter]: That's not even mentioning a potential heatstroke. [The camera zooms to Silva's serious face.] Which means we need to wear appropriate hats to protect our heads, and carry plenty of water with us. Because, what are the leading causes for tourist accidents on our mountains? [She takes a pause with an arched eyebrow, like she's waiting for an answer from the audience.] Insufficient amount of water and inappropriate clothing, especially, of course, footwear. Our guide warned us that we should by no means underestimate the mountain. Many people end up mistaking hiking on Velebit for an easy stroll in the park, and end up dehydrated or confused from sunstroke, stumbling off the track, and when the rescue search finds them, it's too late.

Hrvoje [in the background]: And no, flip-flops aren't appropriate footwear, no matter what the Czech would say.

Lorena [giggling]: Hrvoje, we'll need to cut this out so we don't get canceled for xenophobia.

[The camera's eye zooms out from Silva's face. Lorena is smiling, and even Silva is trying to hide her smile behind the wine glass, but it's unsuccessful. In the background, we can catch a glimpse of Marina, still frowning.]

Lorena: So. [She's counting on her fingers.] We have to wake up early. Then a big breakfast. Carry tons of water—fun fact, that'll be our biggest weight on the hike, heavier, even, than the equipment we're dragging with us! Hats. Plenty of sunscreen. Did I forget something?

[Silva is shaking her head no.]

Lorena [puts her fingers down]: Ideally, we'll be ready to start at seven o'clock. We're going to cheat for the first part of the trip with the help of our dear rental's host—link in description, of course—and use a car. He'll drop us at the point where we can reach the trail for Strogir from the main road, rather than starting our ascent from the town. From that position, hiking toward Strogir should take approximately an hour, maybe even an hour and a half, since we're taking lots of pics and videos, so we can showcase to you, our dear viewers, all of the natural beauties waiting for us on the hike. Patrons will, as usual, have access to all the unedited B roll footage, so if you want to see bonus material, follow the link in the description and drop us a coin so we're able to continue doing these adventures for you. [Lorena smiles and lightly shrugs, like she's uncomfortable mentioning money.]

Lorena [continuing]: On our way to Strogir, we will pass through the infamous Turkish Door. [She turns toward Marina.] Mara, what do you think, are we also going to find the portal to the other world where fairies are hiding the gold, just like the Turks did, once upon a time?

[The camera zooms in on Marina, who looks up from the phone in her hand, still slightly frowning, but when she notices that the lens is facing her directly, the look on her face transforms into a secretive smile. It's a face that sing-songs to the viewer, "I know something that you don't."]

Marina: Honestly, more than fairies and gold, I'm worried that we'll end up like those Turkish forces that broke their necks during the fall from the mountain.

Hrvoje [in the background]: Booooooo, party pooper.

Marina [continuing]: And, even if we do find the secret, hidden treasure, the government would probably confiscate it from us. [She winks to the viewers.] That's why you can be sure—on the off chance that we do find the gold, be it Turkish or fairy gold, on top of Strogir or somewhere else on this magnificent mountain—that the discovery will not be documented on video. [She hunches over her laptop, with a wide smile.] It'll be up to you, when watching this vlog, to guess whether we found it or not. [She shrugs and leans back in her chair with nonchalance.] The big hint will be whether I quit my job or not. [At that, she bursts into loud laughter, but her eyes are solemn, without mirth.]

Lorena [in the background, while the camera zooms out from Marina's face.]: Okay, you'll have to cut this out, obviously. [She claps her hands and the camera is now showing Silva and her again.] Back to the important things. What were we talking about before this little digression?

Silva: The Turkish Door.

Lorena: Oh, yeah! So, after we pass the Turkish Door—which is just a smallish stone monolith that rises from the mountain like a tooth, creating a tight pass—we have Strogir, a bigger stone monolith. It's perfect for alpinists, who love to climb it, but unfortunately, none of us is an alpinist. But you can be sure, if we catch just a glimpse of a golden glint, I'll learn how to climb the mountain on the spot, even without gear. [She laughs.] After that, we'll continue the hike toward mountain hut Alan. But! [She takes a dramatic pause and turns toward Silva.] We won't go straight to Alan, will we?

Silva [shakes her head]: No. Lying northwest of Strogir, there's an abandoned ropeway station and in the surrounding area we can find miniscule, but still populated villages. Those kinds of places can be rich with folk tales just waiting to be documented.

Lorena: And, of course, there's plenty of deserted villages. In case you don't know, people living in this region used to have so-called shepherds' huts on the mountain. During the summer, they would take their herds and go live there up high, and then at the end of the summer season, they would descend back to their coastal homes. So, we'll definitely explore the area for these desolated huts, while, as Silva mentioned, also searching for the populated places with locals living bravely in the middle of nowhere. We're taking sleeping bags and ultralight hiking tents, and we're filming this experience, just for you, dear viewers! The next day, we'll go back east to Alan. The adventure awaits us!

[Lorena's gaze slips from the lens to somewhere above the camera.] I think this should be enough for now. Later, on the hike, we can film Slobodan who'll tell his own anecdote and who can go a bit more into the history and the use of the ropeway.
Hrvoje [in the background]: I agree. The lighting's changed drastically.
Marina [in the background]: Are you sure you guys really want to get off the...[the video cuts off.]

5. Transcript of the video footage of the hike toward the Turkish Door, July 22nd, 2024. The image shows Lorena, with a dark blue fishing hat and a gigantic hiking backpack—which looks bigger than her—a red, rolled-up sleeping bag fixed atop. Her skin is glistening from the sunscreen and sweat breaking out in large drops trickling down her forehead. The crimson marks are clearly visible on her neck, collarbone and arms, much angrier than in the prior video. She's panting, trying to catch her breath, puffed up and bent at her waist. An older man is standing by her side, Slobodan Relić. The extremely thin and tanned hiker has his own backpack with a rolled-up sleeping bag and a tent hooked to it. He has a baseball cap and sunglasses. Behind them, the camera angle shows looming pine trees and tall grass, while the two stand on the broken rocks of a narrow mountain path.

Hrvoje [in the background, also panting heavily]: We've barely been walking for twenty minutes, Lori.
Lorena [straightens up with a tired smile]: Yes, yes, wisecrack. [She takes a deep breath. For a moment, the camera moves away from her and the mountain guide and catches Marina and Silva, farther along the path that continues to climb upwards steeply, the women leaning on the huge stones in the shade of the green trees. They'd left their overflowing backpacks with ultralight tents hooked to them by their feet. Marina is drinking from her metal

water bottle, and Silva is wiping sweat from her face, looking toward the camera. After that short image, the camera comes back to Lorena and Slobodan.]

Lorena [with a deep breath, focusing]: Okay, I think I can start.

Hrvoje [in the background]: Then go, I'm already filming so your faithful followers can see how such a short hike managed to destroy you.

Lorena [Shows her middle finger to Hrvoje, but there's a true smile on her face. It doesn't look like she's resenting Hrvoje's comment. Then she lowers her hand and her face changes from joyful to a camera-worthy smile, the one reserved only for her followers.]: While we walk and enjoy this beautiful day and our view, our mountain guide here, Slobodan Relić, is going to tell us a most curious tale. [She points to the man standing by her side, and the camera zooms closer to his amused face.] It is said that the Relić family had once been blessed by Velebit's fairies.

Slobodan [nodding, with the trained smile of a professional guide, showing a few gaps among his teeth]: Oh, yes, yes. Any horse that the family possessed, it was always a great horse. The best horse in this region. All thanks to the fairy. The story says that there was a Relić who found an injured fairy, here on Velebit, and helped her out. After getting better, to show gratitude, she blessed his horses so that, whichever he buys, it would always be the best horse, and it sort of runs in the family.

Lorena [her face only in profile, looking at Slobodan while he talks]: Why horses? Our viewers could be disappointed, expecting a gift of gold. After all, some say that the treasure on Strogir is fairy gold.

Marina [out of the shot]: Motherfucker! Fuck, shit, fuck!

Silva [out of the shot]: It's good, good, all fine, she's gone.

[The camera swiftly cuts toward the two women. They're both standing, now far from the stones which they were leaning against moments before. A quick, blurry movement of a yellowish tail-end is visible for a second while it disappears into the greenery.]

Hrvoje [in the background, intrigued]: Was that a snake?

Marina [turns toward the camera, hands on her hips]: Yes, of course it was a fucking snake.
Silva: But it's gone, we've probably scared it more than it's scared us.
Lorena [out of the shot]: Okay, so, nothing we didn't know before. We need to be extra careful where we sit down and of each step we take.
[Marina rolls her eyes. Her face screams "pissed off". Two dark butterflies are flying around her, and if she didn't look annoyed, you could say that the image is idyllic. The camera moves from her, back to Lorena and Slobodan. Lorena isn't happy anymore, and Slobodan is shaking his head.]
Lorena [returning to her previous smile]: After this thrilling interruption, let's get back to what we were saying. We were talking about horses. [The last part is directed to Slobodan.]
Slobodan: Horses, horses... oh, yes, the fast horses were like a golden treasure. To the people of the village Dundović Pod, at least. At that time, folks were living as nomads on the mountain. And in addition to herding, they were also transporting logs from the mountain. Fir and spruce. They were dragging it down Velebit, to the sea. Before the construction of the ropeway, the remains of which we're going to visit today, it was a job done by wagoners, so they needed good horses. The Dundović family were legendary wagoners, and the Relić family was famous for having the best horses, all thanks to the fairy.
[The camera zooms out from his face and the angle catches an attentive Lorena.]
Lorena [turns toward the camera lens and then continues]: Another thing we're planning, after the ropeway station, is searching for as many of the shepherd's huts as we can. And if we're lucky, we'll stumble upon the *mirila* too.
Slobodan: Luck will have nothing to do with it, I'm going to show them to you.
Lorena [laughing]: That doesn't sound adventurous enough for our audience. We're going to cut this out. [She gets serious again,

talking directly to the camera.] What are the mirila, you're probably asking yourself. [She's pointing her finger toward the camera, signaling for it to zoom closer to her flushed face.] You've heard by now about the nomadic life people used to lead here, between the life down on the coast, and the life up on the mountain. Cemeteries were situated down there, of course. But what if someone died while they were up here? Far away from the cemetery? Well, in that case, people would bring the deceased down the mountain. When the carriers got tired, though, they would lower the deceased down to the ground, and they would put two rocks in that exact spot, one by the head, and one by the feet, marking the resting place of the corpse. [While she talks, she lifts her arms and moves one to the side when she says *head*, and the other at *feet*, leaving an empty space between her palms for the body.] Later, they would pave the place between those two rocks, so now we have these funeral monuments as a part of Velebit's cultural heritage.

[The camera zooms out from Lorena's face and includes Slobodan again, who's nodding.]

Lorena: So many fascinating things await us, but first, we need to get to the Turkish Door. [She winks at the camera.] It's time to continue this adventure. [With a heavy sigh, she wiggles under the straps of her backpack.] I really hope we're close to this door.

Slobodan [to Lorena]: I'm not sure it's smart to publish this clip, you know I have nothing to do with the Relić family apart from my surn... [the video cuts off.]

6. Transcript of the video footage of the hike toward the Turkish Door. The angle is catching Lorena's back while she climbs over huge stones, overgrown with brambles. The path is steep and breaks through the tall trees providing shade. The crags are visible through the trees. The group walks in a single file because the path is otherwise too narrow. Ahead of Lorena we can see Marina, who walks behind Silva, and leading the way is Slobodan. The footage is shaky and rocks constantly,

because Hrvoje is shooting at the same time as walking. For the first few minutes, the only thing audible on the footage is panting and ragged breaths, mostly Hrvoje's, because he's the closest to the mic.]

Hrvoje [gasping]: Goo... Google had... said... by the... esti...mate... we should've... already... been at... the pass... lies... just lies... but here... I want... you... to see... what it actu...ally... looks... like... this... hike...
[The camera shakes once, violently, and the angle slips from Lorena and her huge, swelled backpack which looks like it will explode at any moment, and starts rolling in free fall, stopping with a loud crack and a shout, easily identifiable as Hrvoje's voice. For a few moments, the image shows earth and rocks, hazy and unfocused. Suddenly, a fuzzy and cylindrical body with tiny legs lands on the camera lens, a part of its wing visible only at the edge of the angle.
Hrvoje [out of the shot, in a painful tone]: Fuck! Fuck your bleeding sun!
Two women's voices are overlapping out of the shot, worried: Jesus, Hrvoje, are you alright?! [Marina shouts.] The camera! [Lorena shouts.]
[The butterfly flies away. The camera shakes and starts lifting from the ground. For a moment, Hrvoje is visible sitting on the rocks, out of focus, grasping at his knee bathed in a flow of red, and then the video cuts off.]

7. Transcript of the video footage of the hike toward the Turkish Door, continuation of the previous clip. Hrvoje, in his blue, sweat-stained T-shirt, stands in the shade of a tree in his knee-length brown shorts, pointing with his right hand at the white gauze covering his left knee. His right palm is also wrapped in white. At his legs is his backpack, a big black Deuter, completely new.]

Lorena [in the background]: Can you tell us what happened?
Hrvoje [with an amused, but shy smile]: I learned two things. A) It's not smart to shoot and hike at the same time, especially on a path this steep where I need to be extra careful walking, and B) it's not smart to hike in shorts. [Hrvoje bursts out laughing, showing his white teeth.] Actually, I should've said that I'd decided to give a gift of blood to the mountain, so it's good to us. Or, at least, to me, since I was the one who bled. [He shrugs, still amused.] But, seriously, 'tis only a scratch. And our dear Marina always carries a whole pharmacy with her so we've managed to fix the problem right away.
Marina [The camera turns toward her and catches her unamused face under the wide-brimmed straw hat. Her shades hide her eyes.]: The word you're looking for is "thanks". And I only have the basics. Band-aids and gauze, in the case, well, something like this happens. [She points in his direction, as if emphasizing her words.]
[The angle of the camera moves 360° toward Lorena, who's shooting this clip. Her glistening red face is in extreme close-up for a few moments.]
Lorena: Once, I fell so hard while we were walking like this in some forest on the island of Brač, the skin of my palms was shredded, there was blood everywhere as if who knows what happened. We didn't have anything with us to wrap my palm with. Since then, Marina's always been prepared.
[The camera moves from Lorena's face and shows the rest, including Silva and Slobodan who are patiently waiting nearby. Slobodan is the only one who doesn't look tired, but even his face is covered with sweat drops. Silva, on the other hand, looks like she's glad for the unexpected respite.]
Lorena [continuing in the background]: Thankfully, the camera doesn't seem broken. And Hrvoje says he can walk. So, we're continuing on with our expedition for the hidden treasure.
Silva [only partially in the shot]: Maybe this is a sign from some gods to stop... [the video cuts off.]

8. Viber messages Hrvoje and Saša exchanged during the short rest after Hrvoje's fall.

[Photo of the bloody, torn knee in close-up.]

guess who was super smart
8:48

Saša
Oh, fuck me, are you okay??
What happened?
8:49

I filmed and walked at the same time lol
8:49

Saša
Very smart, indeed. What now?
Does it hurt badly? Can you walk?
Is this ep going toend at the hospital?
8:50

no,no, I'm fine. Scratched my palm and knee
8:51

hurt my elbow trying to save the camera
8:51

so I landed badly on my hand. But I'm completely fine.
8:51

I'll be okay. I don't need a hospital. Marina carries first aid, a bit of sterile gauze and I'm good to go.
8:52

Saša
Don't you dare stop texting.
8:53

of course, while there's coverage
8:53

and rightnow, I see it keeps steady :D
8:53

Saša
Good luck with the rest of the hike, and please, please, this better not end with Karla and I cringing while hgss is rescuing you on the tv like you're some stupid tourist.
8:54

hahaha dont worry
9:03

I left my flipflops at home
9:03

need to go, we'll continue our walk for the turkish door. I hope they're close.
9:04

we were like already supposed to be there, but apparently we're slow as snails
9:04

I'll send a pic as soon as we get there, thistime without blood :D
9:04

fingers crossed
9:05

love u
9:05

Saša
Love you too! Sorry, I was on a call, my parents are inviting us for lunch the sunday after you're back.
9:37

So? Where is this promised pic? Did you get to it? Let me see that thing.
9:38

Hrvojeeee, honeeey, where are youu
9:38

Where's the pic, are you really still walking?
9:39

Or did you get hurt again? So now you're embarrassed?
9:39

I hope you didn't kiss the ground again. You're only permitted to kiss me he he he
9:39

Is it bc of the reception? Did you finally lose it and I'm sending these messages in vain?
9:40

I'm going to assume you're out of reach, I see the messages are undelivered. When you get reception and see this spam, call me so I know you're okay!
9:41

9. Transcript of video footage at the Turkish Door. In the image, you can see the glare of the sun reflecting from the white stone, tall trees and the view of the wide, bright blue, glittering sea, dotted with brown, bare islands, and at the horizon, the sea touching the vivid azure of the open sky. The camera turns from this beautiful view and focuses on a big piece of phallic stone sticking out of the mountain. Between that stone and the rest of the mountain is a narrow pass overgrown with green underbrush. Marina, with her wide straw hat, stands close to the pass obscured in the greenery, but on the other side from Hrvoje, who's already passed through. By the angle of the camera, I'm guessing that Hrvoje stands on some sort of raised ground, a bit to the side, where he has a good view of the Turkish Door and the people going through the pass.

Hrvoje [in the background, quietly]: I have the higher ground. [louder]: Okay, I'm filming!
You can start going through. [in a dramatic tone]: Dun, dun, duuuun! And first to come through the Door is Marina.
[Marina walks from the shade through the pass and waves at the camera, while Hrvoje keeps running the commentary. After her, Silva goes next, hunched under her backpack, clutching her straps. Her eyes go over the white monolith on one side, then she turns toward the mountain, and points to the hiking mark left on the stone. Hrvoje follows her movement and zooms on the words, clearly visible in the video, "TURSKA VRATA", the first word, *Turkish*, in red, the other word, *Door*, in white. The usual colors of trail markings. All of the path is very visibly marked, which I checked when I hiked this same trail with Saša in the company of the hiking club Kamenjarić.
The camera zooms out and shows Slobodan passing through, seemingly amused by the group's behavior. He even waves at the camera. Lorena ends up last, still staying on the other side of the pass, her head turned toward the tall monolith, her face clearly radiating happiness. Maybe because she was truly excited by a rock,

or maybe because that had meant they were near Strogir. Her thin blue shirt is covered in dark circles from sweat.]

Lorena [loudly, her hands in the air]: Woooo! The Turkish Door!
Hrvoje [mumbling, but the mic catches his words because of how close he is to it]: More like a Turkish Dick than a Door. [even quieter]: By the way, don't snitch me to Saša, but I touched the Turkish Dick while I was passing through.
[Lorena turns toward the rest of the group, waiting for her on the other side of the narrow pass. At the exact moment when she starts walking through the so-called door, the footage suddenly starts disappearing. The distortion of light and shadows transforms it into broken pixels, constantly shifting, superimposing one image above the other, leaving the effect of double vision. The stones creating the pass—the monolith and the mountain—change to the gray-white snow of a broken television programme. On the audio, you can hear a loud cacophony like the song of an untrained choir whose words are unintelligible. When the image finally stops shifting, the noise completely cuts off, and the frame freezes on Lorena as if it were a photo. That frame is extremely short, a millisecond, and the video abruptly cuts off. To see the last frame clearly, you need to slow down the video and hit pause, just like me. And, even with that, and with all the existing photo editing programs, I can't clean it up. I can only try my hardest to describe what it shows.
The colors in the frame are washed out, and Lorena's body is stretched out to an unnatural height. Around her, the pixelated pass resembles open jaws. Lorena's face is in profile while she looks toward the monolith. The corrupted video file creates shadows behind Lorena, a spilled dark color like monochrome wings, leaving the impression of the Rorchach test. Or the wings of the Satyr butterfly. Same as with the butterfly, if you look at the image too long, you'll be convinced that the small eyes at the

tops of the wings are looking back at you. Lorena's own eye in the profile is black, but shining, like a burning piece of coal, and from her open mouth leaks the color of spring dandelion, flowing though the image and disappearing in the depths of the opened Turkish Door.]

10. Transcript of the video footage, I'm assuming near Strogir. The video file is too corrupt to be sure. On the audio, you can mostly hear white noise, periodically interrupted by words the speakers of which I've tried to identify as best as I could.

[The colors are mostly browns, green and ashen, and the image is so grainy it's hard to say what is being recorded. One brown mass resembles a giant tooth that could pass for Strogir. Instead of the blue for the sky or the sea, dark grays and black shades dominate the footage. The image skips like a series of photos stuck during a screening, a bit like stop motion. Within the browns, we can glimpse humanoid shapes. One of the shapes has rust on their head, so I can safely say that's Marina. Her face is turned toward the camera, but it's completely blurry, as if someone has smeared drawn lines with acetone. The other figure has a black cloud around her head—that would probably be Silva with her dark, disheveled locks. She waves her arms and points toward, I'm guessing by their position, the sky. The white noise is broken up by Hrvoje; I'm pretty sure that's him.]

Hrvoje: ... kh... just manifested... dark... [unintelligible for a few seconds] shelter... how is that... [unintelligible for a few seconds] the camera is fucking...
A bodiless woman's alto, so I'm going to assume it's Marina [out of the shot; at this moment, the direction of camera starts lowering so we can see the shape of blurry feet]: ...what the devil... let me see...
Hrvoje [in the background]: ... don't understand...

A woman's voice of a higher register, could be Lorena or Silva [out of the shot, in a questioning intonation]: ...watching?
Slobodan [out of the shot, disturbed]: Careful, careful...
The low woman's voice, probably Marina [out of the shot]: ...what? Sloboda...
The higher woman's voice, Silva or Lorena [out of the shot]: ...no signal... since the door... clouds... mistake... return?
The higher woman's voice, Silva or Lorena [out of shot]: ...absolutely not... from sugar... video... it'll be great... the audience loves...
Hrvoje [out of the shot]: Lorena, watch out... [The video cuts off.]

11. SMS message Hrvoje tried to send to Saša. The message managed to get through in the morning of the day when the tourists found Hrvoje.

> the service is suddenly shit. Just wanted to say we passed strogir. lori is crazy, she wants to cotninue for the ropeway, but we hav e a summer stomr brewing over our heads.there's a chance it'll get harder to check in, but i hope i'll have reception in the m hut when we finally drag our asses tehre. sending sms bc i know it'll be easier to get through to you when i catch the signal somewhere.

12. SMS message Hrvoje tried to send to me. The message managed to get through in the morning of the day when the tourists found Hrvoje.

> on the way for the r way.it could rain. lori thinks it'll be a good story for the video. i hope that the msg will get either to you or sasa.

13. SMS message Hrvoje tried to send to Saša. The message managed to get through in the morning... oh, you already know when.

> one woudl think that the guide knows sides of the wordl and manages on the terrain. lol maybe we'll need HGSS. sooorry! if the msg goes throguh to you, call them, fck slobodan.

14. Hrvoje's note in the notes app on his phone. He frequently used the app to write down ideas for his podcast, things he didn't want to risk forgetting later, impressions, thoughts, details and such, so he could use them for inspiration.

Does croatia have a cursed mountain? Research it.
Even if there's no stories about cursed mountains, this trip could make a good case. I know I'm pissed off right now, but this will make a good story once we get back home.

Note to all who plan to visit Velebit—Slobodan Relić is a horrible mountain guide. The guy is a scam.
Second note to all who want to visit Velebit in search of a hidden treasure—don't.

The thing that gets to me most are the fucking clouds. They just manifested out of thin air, literally. They can't just materialize in the middle of a bright sunny day. Can they? Research it.

Potential cold open of the first episode: Did you know the Velebit is filled with deserted houses, gaping open, empty and dark, covered in plant life strangling them from the inside out?—needs more brainstorming, the sentence is too wordy and clumsy.

Remember that the path is completely overgrown, even more than on the way to the turkish dick—wild fruit trees grow everywhere, in thick clusters. I can't recognize plants for shit, but I do trust Silva, at least over our dear guide. And she says we're fighting against dogwood, pomegranate, and hawthorn trees, catching at our clothes with their branches. The trees are so dense, I feel like I'm lost in the rainforest. The thorny branches have scratched me all over, I think I look like someone who was beaten with switches all day at a bdsm dungeon.

How much until some inhabited place? Who knows. Slobodan says not too long, but Slobodan knows shit about our location.
When you get home, open up google maps and try to find where we were led to by this idiot. Phone still has no bars. Slobodan has some old-school printed map, but he obviously doesn't know how to read it, and neither do any of us, bc we're constantly walking in circles, finding the same abandoned ruins of shepherds' huts, hidden under the lichen and thorns. They look unamused. They look angry. They look dead. It's funny how much some miserable dilapidated huts can radiate with malicious energy. This'll be a good story for the podcast. If I ever come back. Lol At least it hasn't started raining yet.

Are Velebit's ticks carriers for some weird diseases? Research it. If I die on this mountain bc of some stupid tick that latched onto my calf to suck blood, I'm going to return as a ghost and haunt Slobodan for the rest of his loser life.

Sooner or later, someone will step on a snake. The grass is simply too tall. Marina mentioned that at least five times while we were walking. Nobody wants to think about that. Slobodan is the first in the line, hitting the ground with a stick he found. Marina is not impressed. Neither am I.

The inhabited village Slobodan promised us are two houses in the middle of nowhere. At least they have water. But they don't have electricity nor signal. They've never even heard of the internet. Two families live here. Two women and two guys, very heteronormative. On average, I would say they're 65. How fucked they are in their heads to live here, I have no idea. But they look strong, like they could break the rocks from the mountain with bare hands. One of the women has a real, living snake for a pet (note for future me: insert an obvious euphemistic joke here). Allegedly, the snake loves to sunbathe on the roof of their house, and we've been told not to worry, it doesn't love the taste of human meat. Ha. Ha.
The names of our host couple are Ida or Aida, not sure, and Bilal, which sounds like a demon, but apparently it's not a demon but of Turkish origin. They offered us food and drinks. Some sort of hard cheese, dry figs, raw zucchini in vinegar, pomegranate, and heavy-duty rakija. Slobodan says that the rakija is tasty, but so strong he could use it to disinfect wounds. I hate rakija so I passed. Others are eating out of politeness. To be honest, my stomach churns from the stench of the cheese. Remember that smell—strong and syrupy purulent—slipping into the nostrils and tickling the brain to the point of vomiting. Remember Marina's face—her pursed lips and frown—while she was chewing on a piece of cheese by force. Thank gods for my sandwiches and my backpack with the thermal bottom keeping the cool of the melting ice. That could soon become a problem. But, we should get to Alan tomorrow, so I don't think I'll starve before then, I hope.

Silva interrogated both couples and recorded their tales of lost turks and fairies with her zoom recorder.* One of the stories is particularly bloody. It goes like this: a group of Turkish men stumble upon a werewolf on the mountain. The werewolf's only skin on the bones and the blood in his veins, starving and crazy from the sun. The starving werewolf hunts them one by one, devouring each of the caught men in their entirety, from the tendons and entrails, to the bones he gnaws. The men turn to morsels left on a plate, for the werewolf to lick them clean, so not even that stays behind. His stomach gets bursting full like he's pregnant, but at least he's not hungry anymore. He eats everyone except for one young man, whom he keeps alive. Why? They don't know. The tale doesn't tell us that. Only that he keeps the young man alive. Like the guy is a Ken doll, or maybe a treat for later, when the werewolf gets hungry again. After that story, I felt nauseated so I went outside to get some air. The couples continued telling tales to Silva. While I was getting out of the house, I heard them mention the gold and where it's hidden by the fae folk. But I don't want to hear any new stories. Not now. Not until I get back home. Silva's having the time of her life, at least. I can't remember seeing her happier than this.

Marina tried to film, testing the camera, but if she manages to squeeze any sort of footage out of it, kudos to her. Something's damaged after my fall. In the worst possible moment. The footage is completely useless, even weird as fuck—the one she filmed in this village especially. She freaked herself out. Doesn't matter. I see that Lori is recording everything with her phone. She's walking around the "village", her phone out. I should also do that, but my phone memory's full. I could erase a few videos and photos to make space, but I don't want to. I don't know why, but I feel this irrational dread that if I erase old videos I'll forget Saša and Karla. Anyway, it's not important. Lori will have all of the footage on her phone, I could ask her for the material if it turns out I need it.

My knee aches. Not too much to be a problem, but it's a sort of a blunt pain pulsing in my kneecap while I walk. It gets on my nerves. Bilal offered me some homemade plant-based ointment for aching bones, but Marina dragged me off to the side and forbade me to accept anything from these strangers, since we have no idea

what's mixed in there and I could have an allergic reaction. She's green in the face, probably from that rotten cheese she ate. She wants to get away from this place as soon as possible, but Silva is not finished yet. Marina is still freaking out, probably bc of that stupid video footage. But ever since we came to this village, there's something restless inside of me, as if my internal organs want to leak through my nostrils and my mouth.
To be honest, I think I'm also scared shitless bc of that freaky footage.

***[Silva's Zoom H2n recorder is lost to us, just like Silva.]**

15. SMS message Hrvoje tried to send to Saša. You already know when it ended up getting delivered. I'm guessing that he wrote this on the first day of the hike, June 22nd, while they were in the currently unidentified village, so I'm putting it chronologically here. But also, I have no idea if that's correct. He could've written this at any point before his battery ran out.

I would live with you even on the mountain, in the middle of the empty space, where only you and I exist, and no one else.

16. SMS message Hrvoje tried to send to Saša. You already know when it got delivered.

but I would still like us to have the internet and a water source.

17. SMS message Hrvoje tried to send to Saša...

plus Karla would kill us if we weren't able to pick up our phone calls.

18. Transcript of the video footage. I'm assuming it was filmed in the currently unidentified village, and that it's the footage Marina filmed when testing the camera, the one mentioned in Hrvoje's note. Although, in the meantime we've managed to visit a few of the inhabited villages in the vicinity of the trail where the group got lost (see my sketch),* and none of them has a couple with the names Hrvoje wrote in his notes. The fact that we can't find (A)Ida and Bilal is the reason why some believe that Hrvoje was already under mental duress when he wrote his notes on the village, probably hallucinating due to the lack of water. That sounds too far-fetched to me, especially because these notes were very coherent, unlike his later writings, where we can follow his mental breakdown.

*we as in Saša and I—we researched this area with the help of the previously mentioned hiking club Kamenjarić after the police and the HGSS (Croatian Mountain Rescue Service) didn't have anything useful for us.

[The footage is short and distorted. The shapes are shattered into hundreds of fuzzy pixels. The movement of the camera is slow. The vivid green color is spilled all over the sky; the treetops of the large trees sway restlessly as if seen through a prism of invisible smoke in the air. The shot moves from the trees to the small stone house and the footage suddenly starts to pulsate. The form of the house is blurry, unfocused. The lines are smudged like watercolors spilled on paper. When the footage is sufficiently slowed down, the gaping holes in the house become visible. Something dark dribbles from the holes, greasy like pus. Some kind of a brownish shape, hazy and elongated, is visible on the roof. When the footage is slowed down to a crawl, you can glimpse movement, similar to a hand or a leg motion, but generally, the form is too shapeless to be called a human figure.]

The lower woman's voice, probably Marina [in the background]: What the fuck. [Shaky, but louder.]: Hrvoje? Come here? [Something unintelligible, lost in the noise of the whispering woods.]: ... looking at... lense... not same as... my eyes... seeing.

[In the footage, a new figure shows up in the doorframe of the little house, vague but unmistakably humanoid. They look unnaturally elongated, like stretched-out bubble gum, and on their back we can glimpse some kind of dark mass seemingly bursting out from the figure's both sides. Their legs look broken at the knees and ankles, unnaturally twisted. On their feet there's some kind of footwear that's hard to identify, but it resembles hooves.]

The voice I can't identify, it's neither low nor high, and, when speaking, some of the words break into sound waves: ...loves sunbathing... [Something unintelligible like the susurration of a quick river after heavy rain.]

[The footage skips, cuts off for a moment, and in the next, when the video gets back, the brown mass isn't on the roof anymore. Instead, in its place is just a dark, thin, winding line. The footage skips again and cuts off for a moment. In the next one, when we get the video back, there's a face in extreme close-up, doubled in distortion, with a double pair of flaming yellow eyes, and a double mouth stretched in a wide smile filled with small, sharp, incisor-like teeth. The video cuts off, but not before a quiet cry. Probably Marina's. Maybe Hrvoje's.]

19. Lorena's entry from her dream journal where she tracked her night terrors. It's now very well known that Lorena struggled with nightmares her brain generated in those flimsy moments between sleep and wakefulness, paralyzing her. She would wake up and experience very real terror, unable to move from fear. Unlike children's night terrors, when they wake up screaming but with no memory of what they'd dreamt, Lorena remembered every detail of her living dreams.

23. 6. 2024.

I was awoken by the unexpected weight over my calf, above my cotton pajama pants. An elongated form, fat and muscular, slithers over my skin. A snake, I realize. The fabric crumples while she crawls over my body. I can't move. My feet are frozen, my legs carved stone. I lie on my back on the uncomfortable surface, tied up, squeezed, smashed in the closed hand of a giant. I can't see and I can't hear. Everything is obscured before my open eyes, as if someone had covered me with a black veil, thinking I was dead. Maybe I am. I'm dead stiff. Except for me, the snake is the only other thing that exists in this darkness. I follow her path. She massages my inner thighs and pelvis, slithers over my stomach, between my breasts under which my heart beats frantically.

I want to scream, but I'm afraid to open my mouth. The snake continues her ascend; her lower body wrapped over my legs feels endless. The forked, wet tongue licks the skin of my neck. The mass of her supple body strangles me and it's increasingly harder for me to breathe. The tongue strikes my tightly closed lips. Less and less air gets through my nostrils. The forked tongue pushes between my lips as if she wants to kiss me. My whole body is covered in hot goosebumps. The snake's head is pulling my mouth apart, wanting to open me up. The muscles press at my neck, the force crushes my chest. My soft belly is pierced with pain, as if someone is lazily hitting me with a fist. My lungs cry for air and I can't handle this anymore, tears slip down my cheeks and under the snake's nudging my mouth opens wide like a window to clear the air.

I taste reptile skin, salty and earthy. My throat tenses from the effort and my whole rigid body shakes while the snake fills up the tender void of my esophagus with her length. I use the foreign body to map up my insides. I can feel where my organs start and where they end. I intimately know every millimeter of my stomach. The snake pushes through tissue. The wriggling rope stretches out in my colon. She wraps around my ovaries, squeezes tightly. Unbearable pain flows through me, but my body is still frozen over, my soundless scream caught imprisoned in the soft, long body filling up my mouth. The tongue flicks at my uterus, as if the snake is tasting my insides. The snake tail disappears in my mouth, slips down my tongue like sirupy elderberry juice, choking me. With my mouth free, I scream, but my voice is rough and broken, quiet. My vocal cords have been abused by the passing of the snake. Shredded.

My whole body burns. I'll never be able to move my arms or legs again. Circulation is cut off. I'll lose my limbs. Warm palms touch my wet face. I'm made of salt. It melts on my tongue. A woman's voice breaks through the veil. My skin stings all over me, but the fingers on my arms and feet are slowly twitching as I will them to. Through the darkness I can see the grayish light. Marina's voice is sure, comforting, and the fear is slowly freeing me from its clutches.

I'm starting to be aware of the tight embrace of my sleeping bag. That I can't see far because the thin wall of the tent is right above my face. Marina is by my side, she wipes the tears from me, kisses my cheeks, whispers that everything will be okay. That it was only a dream.

Dreaming awake.

A few minutes have passed since then, I think. I'm not sure. As soon as the paralysis had lifted, as soon as my body had calmed and the goosebumps passed, I wriggled out from the sleeping bag, and in the gloom of the tent I felt for my journal and pen. Marina opened the small torch. My phone claims it's dawn, around 5:50. The morning is near. I wanted to write the dream down as soon as I could to expulse it from my mind. This was one of the worst I've ever had. Even though I've been awake for some time now, the traces of the dream linger on my skin. I feel bloated, irritated. My eyes ache.

It doesn't surprise me that I've had a terror this violent. I almost didn't manage to fall asleep. Not only was the ground hard and uncomfortable, but through the night we could constantly hear eerie echoes of wailing in the mountain. I don't know when it stopped, or if it lasted until dawn. I should get ready quickly and

[the entry stops here without an explanation]

20. The second note on Hrvoje's phone. (In the app, this one is above the previous note, because the most recent ones are always first, but I'm putting it here to keep with the timeline of the events.)

A note for every single living person who could find this information useful—when people offer you accommodation for the night in the middle of nowhere, and you're lost, accept it. If the guide has failed you once, he'll fail you the second time.
Even with the new instructions for getting to Alan, our designated mountain hut, from the "village" we'd found ourselves in, we managed to get lost, again. Marina didn't want to stay in the village, no way in hell. Lorena and Silva were ready to accept Bilal's offer to stay the night, even if that meant all five of us squeezing together in the small almost-living room reeking of rotten cheese and dry figs. Silva was absolutely delighted with the tales she collected. Lori was excited with the lifestyle of the couples, with the human relationship to nature heightened to the max. She said it was very pastoral. That's not really the word I would've used. And neither would have Marina.

I agreed with Marina, wishing to leave as soon as possible, not so much running away from these weird mountain people, as from the discomfort lodged under my skin. Slobodan promised us that we'd only need an hour to get to Alan, where we would be able to get a good night's rest. Lori wanted to please Marina, so in the end, she decided—let's risk the trip to Alan instead of staying in the village.

And that's how we got here. Spending the night in sleeping bags in a wild camp in the middle of the untamed forest overgrown with bramble, with sharp stones instead of soft pillows. My dread rises higher. My skin breaks in goosebumps, as if someone is watching me from the shadows out of reach of the orange glow cast from our small garden lights and campfire. Each time I glimpse behind my back, I can't explain it, but I'm certain that I'll catch the gaze of a predator's reflecting green eyes.

Silva can't shut up about the new folk stories now recorded on her zoom. She says they're remarkably strange. Pure gold for her profession (note for future self—insert a joke here how Silva's found her fairy gold). Honestly, I'm trying to ignore her while she goes on and on, and that's why I'm currently fooling around on my phone, rather than listening to her. The tale about the werewolf and the Turks is still buzzing in my head. I don't need that before going to sleep in a tent erected at a wild camp site in the middle of fucking nowhere.

Slobodan seems drunk. Probably from that stupid rakija, who knows how many glasses he's downed. Or he's simply too old so one's managed to fuck him up. He was rambling about how one of the women in the village had donkey legs. Hooves and all. That, while he was taking a leak behind some tree, he saw her taking off her shoes and hiking up her skirts, and that she let him see her legs on purpose. That she winked in his direction. He's talking nonsense, but the more he talked, the paler Marina got. She looked at me with significance. I reall y hope that the dude speaks underthe influence of rakija. And that he didn't spy on a poor elderly woman while she was changing her clothes.

Remember—as if I'll ever be able to forget it—that, all of a sudden, an accordion started playing while our campfire was slowly dying down. It plays somewhere in the distance, and its music shatters over the jagged mountain tops, pouring over us like an avalanche. Maybe someone from the village we left behind took out the instrument and now they're playing. It's not like they have a lot in lieu of entertainment. They don't even have the internet. The accordion isn't the worst. It's just irritating. The noise it makes is awful even in capable hands, and this one sounds as if someone has no idea what they're doing. But that would've been easy to ignroe. But no. the worst part is the singing. If the howling we're hearing could even be called that. Polyphonic. Vocalizing. With no recognizable words. The song bounces around us like an echo. Research what kind of, certainly natural, sounds in the mountain can create this effect, because there's no way that it's really someone singing and playing.

Slobodan says, trembling like a branch, that it's cursed souls we're hearing. Too bad that Silva agrees with him. The betrayal.

I can't sleep. The accordion is not stopping its wailing, nor are the dead souls. It's like I'm listening to the A24 soundtracks of women vocalizing on repeat. I hate it. I'm afraid. My sleeping bag is constricting and the blue light of my phone doesn't help. Anything could hide in the darkness on the other side of the tent. Remember how you scrolled through videos, calming yourself with the visions of some other life. It didn't help. I still can't fall asleep. Silva doesn't have this type of problem, she's sleeping by my side without a care in the world. She even snores a bit. She doesn't mind the creepy ass song, nor the light of my phone. Bless her. I want her brain.

We don't know where Slobodan is. Note for future self—be mindful when you speak about him in the future, hide your animosity. Erase everything negative for the episode.

Remember—that feeling of unadulterated dread gripping your body when you saw the ritual stones. At that moment, you understood, on your own skin, the true meaning of the phrase to freeze from fear. I think that, for a moment, my soul left my body, disassociating from the adrenaline surge. Even now, hours later, my hands are still shaking while writign this. But I need to type it out from my brain. I need to get rid of these feelings somehow.

I don't know when I managed to fall asleep. I remembered constantly twisting and turning, counting every fucking rock under our tent, while sweating like a pig. My ears rang with the echo of the mountain's song. I was expecting that, at any given moment, something, or someone, would crash down on our tent, shred it to pieces, and chop me up for barbeque. I was mostly expecting a feral boar charging the tent and accidentally slaughtering me with its tusks like Robert Baratheon. (Are there any boars on Velebit? Research it.)

But I must have fallen asleep from exhaustion, because at one point I remember thinking how there's a rock painfully stabbing me straight into my spleen, and in the next moment I was awoken by Silva's scream. That had been an effective awakening.

I scrambled out of my sleeping bag and the tent before my brain even loaded to full consciousness, guided more by my instinct than anything else. It was still almost dark. Not the pitch-black of the deep night, but the gloom of the early dawn, when everything is bathed in thick grayness. Silva's shape was easy to recognize, but I had to open the torch on my phone to see her better. Marina and Lori also got out of their tent. Later, they told us they were already awake at that point, because of Lori's night terror.

Silva was awoken by her full bladder. She went to take a leak behind a tree, following the light of her phone. She was supposed to pass Slobodan's tiny triangular tent. The tent was missing. She thought she'd made a mistake. But no matter which way she turned, she could only see our two tents. And then she saw the thing which made her shout, rousing us.

At the place where Slobodan's tent was supposed to be, there's now two familiar ritual stones. Between the stones, there is emptiness. Empty space resembling the length of a fully grown person. One of the stones has a carved circular symbol. We all know what it means. We all saw stones like this when Silva showed us the photos she found on the internet. Mirila. The stones that were put down when the carriers were dragging a corpse down the mountain, to mark the place where the dead had lain.

Slobodan's gone. We called for him, searching around our camp, but we didn't dare to go too far away, so we wouldn't get lost. His name bounced around us, spreading over the mountain. I think that only now, after shouting, I've finally noticed the lack of creepy wailing that bothered us during the whole of last night.

Daylight broke while we stood in the camp, above the mirila stones, like idiots, without any clue what to do next. The sun is also missing. The gray clouds are hanging above our heads. That's probably good. We don't need to worry about heatstroke, though it's still pretty warm.

We're trying to think rationally. When we set up our camp, it was already pretty dark, because of course we were waiting for the last possible minute to accept that, yes, we were indeed lost, again, and we won't get to Alan. In the dark we probably didn't see that we were putting our tents so close to the funeral stones. We probalby misremembered Slobodan's choice of spot. And he probably got lost when he went to take a leak. His tent could've been carried off by some feral animal.

Or he left us, on purpose, alone in the wilderness for some reason. Maybe the guy is a single-minded homophobe, so this is his way of punishing us (I would bet on this). Maybe somebody paid him to leave us. Maybe he dragged us in circles, purposefully leading us away from civilization and now he's left us to fend for ourselves. Because...

I don't even want to go there. It makes no sense. We have no idea what to do, but we agree that our best bet would be to pick up our camp and try to get to Alan. I don't want to, but need to, think about how little food and water I have. I should take a pic of Slobodan's mirila, but I'm getting sick just thinking about it. This would've made a spectacular podcast episode. But I don't believe I'll ever get down this cursed mountain.

Silva is blaming herself for Slobodan's disappearance. She says that someone should've shared the tent with him, that we shouldn't have left him alone. I replied it was fucking stupid, and, in that case, that person should've been me, sharing the tent with him, I mean, but that I don't feel guilty. We don't even know what happened. There's a good chance the guy left of his own free will, and that's the reason all his stuff is missing. If a wild hog dragged his tent away, it would've left some trace behind, right?

I could kiss my external phone battery. Note for future self—maybe I could get a brand deal promoting it.

We're hungry, and Silva swears on her name that she can recognize edible plants and wild fruit, because she attended some courses, and she used to pick bear leek in the meadows with her friend. Isn't that something potentially poisonous? Or is there something poisonous that looks like that plant? Research it.

The only thing worse than being lost in the forest in the middle of the mountain is to have explosive diarrhea in the middle of a fucking mountain forest. I don't even know if I want to remember how my ass is irritated and scratched all over because I tried to wipe with leaves, then changed my mind and sacrificed a shirt. RIP Alien shirt, you'll be missed.
I think I'm going to die. I dont know if its going to happen bc of a poison, or from dehydration bc of all the fluids I keep losing from every hole in my body, instead of any getting into me. We had to stop and camp bc I cant walk like this.

Lori also started to vomit, we're fucked. Her vomit is blood red. I hope it's only the color of the berries, and not the actual blood she's hurling out. Her stomach is somehow bloated, bulging like she's pregnant. Marina is ready to find Slobodan and kill the ever loving god in him. Silva is crying, gurgling how sorry she is. How she was sure she identified all the plants correctly, how we shouldn't be this bad.

I'm trying to sleep. But as sson as the night fell, the song and accordion started. Lori's dry heaving, Marina's cursing, and Silva's crying joins in their music. This is going to be hell.

Silva had trouble falling asleep. She sniffled for the better part of the night, for hours, I would guess. I still can't sleep. At leas t the diarrhea stopped. And I can't hear Lori vomiting anymore, so I hope she's also managed to catch some sleep. The only thing I can hear is the music of the cursed souls. Are those the people who perished on the mountain? Who underestimated its power, challenged Velebit and lost their heads?

I know I fell asleep bc I was awoken by the steps going by our tent. I can feel Silva sleeping by my side, and I can follow the rhythm of her deep breathing. My body tensed and I had to open up my phone so its light can banish the dark. I feel the tingling over my skin. I was sure the steps circled the tent, then stopped. That was probably Lori. Or Marina. One of them had to take a leak. Problem is. If it was one of them. They should've already been back. I should hear the steps once more, when passing our tent to get back to theirs. But no matter how much I'm straining to hear something, anything, there's nothing. Not even the lamentation of the souls. I can't hear anything. Not the crickets. Not the steps. Not the vomiting. Just Silva's quiet breathing.

I'm looking at the clock on my display, the slow changes of the minutes. I'm waiting for someone to get back tot he tent after their bathroom break. I should get up, get out, check if the two of them are okay. To be sure ntohing happened. No way. I'm sorry. I hope they're fine. I'm going to watch odl videos to calm down, otherwise I'll start screaming from the tension, and I dont want to wake Silva up.

It's morning. We're all alive and accounted for, except Lori looks even more bloated then the night before. Her stomach is so swollen it looks like she'll burst open at any moment. That can't be normal, and I can see Marina's also worrying. Silva appears to have lost all capacity for worrying and now resembles a puppet with open seams. Lori and Marina claim that they didn't get out of the tent during the night. I'm the only one that heard the steps outside the tent. I feel sick, and this time, it has nothing to do with Silva's berries.

We're walking. Walking. And Walking. I'm tired. I'm hungry. My knee hurts as hell. My legs hurt. I'm thirsty and I want to go home. How is it possible that we can walk so much and get nowhere? Why is it all the same fucking rocks, the same fucking brambles, the same fucking mountain and trees and deserted, derelict shepherd's huts? Thank the gods that no one came to the brightidea to camp inside them.

I was right. We weren't alone. We were never alone. I
I
I dont know how to write this
How to say this, voice it
I cant i cant i cant
I dont know how long ive been shaking
Hes looking at the phone as if he has no idea what it is
He probably doesnt
that s why he left it with me
Or he knows that its useless shit without a signal
But whatuseofthephone
My battery is about to die
Everything else is inthe camp withothers

Onlythephone is with me
And now its also dying
Forgive me

[The end of the notes on the phone.]

21. The entry from Lorena's dream journal.

25. 6. 2024.

All this is just one continuous nightmare I'm stuck in, and I can't wake up, it pours over from one day to the next, so why shouldn't I write it down? Maybe, once I've imprisoned it in my words, I'll finally break out of it and wake up.

First Slobodan, now Hrvoje. It's been a whole day since his disappearance, and I'm waiting for that moment when the mora will lift from my chest, when I'll open my eyes and see Hrvoje sitting opposite me at the campfire. Joyful, as always. Relaxed. We have known each other since our college years, when we met at some party or another. It was an eternity ago.

He went to our bathroom tree and he didn't come back. The mountain swallowed him. As if he were never here in the first place. No trace left. He had said he heard someone walking through our camp during the night. We said he must've imagined it. Maybe he was right. But if that's the case, what could've happened? Do I really want to know? O god, what will I say to Saša?

We went looking for him, as far from the camp as we dared, similar to our search for Slobodan. We didn't go far. We don't want to change the camp's location, to risk Hrvoje missing us. If he's also trying to get back to us. Silva is constantly biting her nails. She sits on the rocks, her gaze hollow. Marina walks around the tents, pulling her hair. Her face is scrunched, and I understand, she's keeping the rageful scream inside of her. I know how hard she's trying to stay quiet. Not to attract attention.

We ate through everything we had. Everything we got from the nice Velebit people. Everything that Silva found for us. Silva believes she poisoned us, but she didn't. Marina and Silva showed no hints of food poisoning. If she'd been at fault, they would have also suffered through the consequences. Hrvoje may have accidentally eaten something wrong, one berry a shade darker than the others, or a bad green leaf tangled with the edible ones, but whatever is wrong with me, it has nothing to do with food.

My belly is rounded, swollen, a ripe watermelon one just needs to knock on for it to split and open up. I feel something pressing inside. Moving. Punching. The snake I swallowed in my dream. She's settled in me and now she's twisting and turning, finding the most comfortable position. I could cry, but Marina is watching me like a hawk, full of fear. I don't want to make her worry any more than she already does. How could I ever explain that my night terror was real, while the reality I live in is just a horrible nightmare I can't wake up from, no matter what?

[The entry on the next page, I believe it's a different day, but unlike the rest, this one isn't dated.]

I don't say this to Marina, but I see her. The same baba whom I met as a kid. She's currently standing near our camp with her green headscarf and sinewy hands. And huge, velvety, earthy brown wings. I have never said this to anyone. Even though it's silly. In nightmares, everything's possible. This whole journal is filled with entry upon entry of unnatural horrors, bizarre moments and absurd images the only purpose of which is to stoke dread. And yet, I never wrote down that the old woman in my nightmares has wings.

Now, I'm writing this for the first time. I'm admitting to what I see. The wings are long, but thin. Like a shadow transformed into a membrane. I can't believe she can fly with those. She reminds me of a butterfly, one who's managed to grow out human limbs and head. Her eyes shine brightly like the sun we haven't seen ever since we passed through the Turkish Door. At least I'm not burning out anymore.

The baba's reaching for me with a hand and calling me. My legs itch from the need to get up, and go to her. Marina is searching for the signal, raising her phone toward the cloudy skies for the thousandth time. Silva's half asleep, catatonic. The tent she shared with Hrvoje is standing empty, the front flap open so any kind of crawlies can enter, but Silva doesn't seem to care.

I wish to go away with the old woman from my nightmares. It would be so easy, I know it. I wouldn't even need to turn around. I would put my hand in hers, and she would drag me deeper into the mountain. To Velebit's core. She would help me take this skin off me like old clothes that have crusted over with years of wear. I wonder, if I do that, will I also get wings to spread? Will I be able to fly high, toward the sharpened mountain tops?

I shake my head. No, I don't want to go. Not yet. I don't want to abandon Marina. Our life makes me happy, our travels and vlogs, our touches and love. Just the thought of me walking away from it opens up an abyss under my heart. I already miss her, and I'm still sitting in the same place, in front of our tent, on rocky ground. Where I can see her struggling to connect with the outside world. Silly, I want to tell her, we're not in that world anymore. The one of phones and the internet. It doesn't exist for us anymore. We only have the mountain, the butterflies and the snakes who nest in wombs.

[Third undated entry.]

And the wolves. I forgot about the stupid wolves. I believed all of them died out long ago, hungry and thirsty, lonely. There's no worse thing than a solitary wolf. Wolves need packs to live.

Hrvoje doesn't look good. His hair is dirty with mud. His eyes are filled with tears. His face is crusty from the salt. He refuses to speak. Marina works hard at comforting him, touching his hand lightly, speaking softly, even though she's scared of the wolf who's not leaving his side. The wolf grins. I hate that shit-eating grin. I would gladly take it off with an ax, but I don't have an ax to pull out from our stuff.

He's looking at me with his huge yellow eyes. Saliva is dripping from his jaw. I know he would gladly eat me if he could. I know it's his biggest wish. To rip out my neck with his canines, gulp down my blood. To gouge out, with his claws, my rounded, feverishly pulsing stomach. The snake feels the predator so close to us. Not even my baba shows up anymore. She's left me alone to deal with this beast.

Hrvoje probably thinks he's imprisoned, but he wields the biggest power here. For whatever reason, the wolf listens to him. Why would he bring Hrvoje back to us, otherwise? Why would he sit with us by the fire, instead of devouring us all?

If nothing else, their arrival brought Silva out of her vegetative state. While Marina is trying with Hrvoje, Silva puts all her efforts into interviewing the two-legged wolf, leaning against the rock, with his long legs stretched out before him. Her recorder is out in front of his face, and the questions aren't stopping, nor are his smug answers. Her eyes are alight with curiosity. Maybe she's finally accepted the truth that we're stuck in the dream, where she has this incredible opportunity to uncover the tales she would never find in the waking world. It's only a question of whether she'll get the chance to get back home to publish them.

I'm waiting for the opportunity to slit his throat. The wolf, I mean, not Hrvoje. I have a blade in my backpack. Once the night falls, and the song of the dead starts to play, I'll use their wails to hide my steps from his sharp hearing. Hrvoje won't mind. If you ask me, he'll thank me.

[The fourth undated entry. This one is written in a different handwriting, which I can identify as Hrvoje's, though his hand was obviously shaking hard while writing, making some parts harder to read. It's also hard to guess how many entries

are actually here because he didn't use any breaks or separators which would clearly distinguish the different days, but given the discoloration of the segments and the handwriting, we're assuming he did write on several occasions, rather than all in one go. We also can't be sure of the chronology of the events, since it's obvious that he wrote things down in a stream of consciousness, instead of following a clear timeline. I'm not even going to mention the authenticity of the events, it's up to you to choose if you're going to believe his records, and to what extent.]

Marina told me that Lori used this notebook to document her night terrors, the worst ones. She told me she sees I'm getting lost, more and more. That I shouldn't let it happen. That I need to remember who I am, what I am, and who waits for me at home (Saša. Karla. Mom and dad. Friends. Uncle and other relatives. My podcast audience. Hahahah audience. Podcast. That's something from another world.) **[This part was stained with dried drops of some liquid, especially the word "audience" that's almost completely smeared, but still legible enough.]**

When she gave me this notebook, Marina openly sobbed. Her hands were bloody, leaving the reddish smear of her fingers on the cover. When was that? Some of the red faded away. Some left traces on my own palms.

I need to remember... what? What do I need to remember? What did she want me to remember?

Remember—the trees aren't moving. The whole point of the trees is that they're fixed to a spot, deeply rooted in the ground. Every time I lie down, I can see the treetops floating over my head like clouds.

Remember—people don't walk on donkey-like hooves. They have soft feet with five little toes like mine. I just need to take my shoes off and I'll see the truth. I can't forget that. Butterflies are just butterflies, flying over flowers, eating pollen, good tiny pollinators.

They don't have tender human skin nor long fingers they'll gladly stick into your eyes if they could.

Remember—everything smells like pomegranates and grass, like worms burrowing in the earth, like salt in the air and dry olives in thorny shrubbery. The nights are pleasantly chill, the days are warm. My fur is muddy and covered in thistles. No. Wrong. I don't have fur. People don't have fur. They have hairs. Mine are constantly up, even now, while I write, because I know he'll

doesn't matter

it's not like he knows how to read.

Remember—at the beginning there were five of us. Slobodan was an okay dude. You could see he knew what he was doing. I can't remember why I was so irritated with him. Circles. We would have walked in circles with him or without him. It wasn't his fault. I know that now. I didn't before. Slobodan. Rererelić. Relić. An okay dude. Remember that. In case someone asks you, so you know how to answer. I asked him if he was to blame for Slobodan's disappearance. I promised him that I won't be mad if he was, that I didn't like Slobodan in the first place, I just want to know the truth. ~~I was already pretty angry about so many things. Slobodan would be a drop in a sea of rage. And fear.~~ He claims he didn't do anything to Slobodan, with his stupid smug grin that's wide enough to show his canines. ~~Each time I see them my left arm itches, that spot under my armpit. And my shoulder. And my inner thigh. Three reasons for anger, right there. Three reasons for fear.~~ Slobodan fluttered away with the butterflies, that's we he says. Maybe. He's not sure. He didn't see it happen. But he suspects the butterflies, they're always the culprits, and if not them, then snakes ~~or wolves, I would add, but I didn't~~. He swears up and down that he didn't even touch Slobodan. I don't know if I believe that. I know now that he followed us from the village. That he was always close to our camp, even before he ~~kidnapped took dragged me~~ even before I got lost and stumbled upon him. The tale from the village says that the werewolf ate all the Turkish men except one young man whom he kept alive. If he's lying, that would mean that Slobodan is being digested at the bottom of the wolf's stomach. That would explain the meat he brought me to eat. He says it's a snake. I've never tried snakes, so I have no idea what they should taste like.

Remember—people can't give birth to snakes. That's biologically impossible. Humans can birth other human beings. Snakes break through into this life from eggs. You couldn't have seen what you believe you've seen. Forget about it.

Remember—Silva was primarily Lorena's friend. We shared a tent, and we shared jokes, but the truth was, we used to only hang out when Lori and Marina organized something for all of us. She didn't betray me with her interest in the wolf tales, with acting like everything was normal, a-okay, like his presence was acceptable or welcome. She too wanted to find something positive in this whole nightmare. She~~'s also afraid~~ was afraid. She was scared for herself, for me, for all of us. She too had loved ones waiting at home for her return. Still, did she have to jump at him like that, her recorder and questions ready? After the first shock over my sudden reappearance with him in tow had passed. Marina had seemed on the verge of tears. Lori was visibly sick. But Silva took out her zoom.

Remember—Lorena ~~is watching~~ watched him with such hatred and he would give back double, showing his teeth. In turn, she would sharpen her knife. Marina was constantly keeping an eye on the two. She would calm Lori down, I would calm him. None of that mattered anymore.

Remember. Remember. Marina told me to remember, but there's so much I want to forget.

Lori writhed in pain. Her screams reverberated, carried in the air. Her stomach pulsed while her back was arching. Marina didn't know whether she should hold her or keep far away from her. ~~Silva had her arms on~~ Silva wasn't with us anymore, remember that, Hrvoje? Instead of Silva, there was an empty space at Lorena's right side. I was standing at least three steps away from her.

Clutching hard at his hairy forearm like a fucking fool, because I didn't know what to do, how to help. How to help a person who's losing a fuck ton of blood between their legs, whole streams of blood drenching the dry ground? What would one do if, in all that red, the small head of a horned viper emerged with its tiny horn on top of the snout? (Is there a specific term for it? For the horn? Research it. Ha ha hahahahah as if I'll ever be back home to google the specific terms for horned viper anatomy.) I'm not sure what I was supposed to do, but I'm certain that it shouldn't have been just standing there, frozen, useless, while Lori, with her whole strength and scrunched up face, pulls out, from her body, a long reptile like it was a stuck tampon. Marina shrieked, and shrieked, and shrieked. Forget the sound of wet wriggles while the snake rolled in the blood-soaked grass. Forget all about it. That was just a nightmare.

~~Whatever you think you've seen, it wasn't Lori breastfeeding a venomous snake, while Marina sits further away, gasping in bloody tears. It's said that women change when they become mothers. You have no idea if that's true, it sounds like a load of bullshit, but Lori surely did change. Or maybe that was all from the toxins in her bloodstream.~~

Remember—water is the best thing in the world, even when it's only old rainwater, filthy and full of microorganisms, surely resulting in new bouts of diarrhea. Maybe it would be best if we all croaked from dehydration. Maybe that would be the most painless death. If you ever get home, don't research how painful it is to die of dehydration because I'm pretty sure that, no matter the results, it would always be less painful than this, now.

Remember—his story. Should I even remember that? Silva's recorder has it neatly collected in its memory, but there's no recorder, no Silva. Was Marina also talking about that when she told me to remember? I wonder. His story is very similar to ours. They also went searching for the treasure. Haha. Fucking treasure. To us, that was just a super cool story we could serve to our faithful audiences who would, in turn, give us some money for the entertainment.

That was the real conversion of the fictional gold into real money. But to him and to six of his friends? I'm not sure which group they belonged to. Romans? Turks? Hajduks? That had been so long ago, he claims he doesn't remember himself ~~or he acts forgetful~~. But what he remembers is the hunger. He remembers walking in his torn opanci on his feet. He remembers the sticks and the clubs and the golden ducats they'd stolen. He remembers that there had been a whole bag full of it, hidden. They came for it one day. Instead of finding their bag, they got lost. Just like us. They passed through the door and got stuck on this side. Silva had asked him whether his werewolf found them then, just like in the villager's tale. His hackles rose at that question and he growled ~~and that sound vibrated in my ribs~~. What happened to them wasn't the fault of the werewolf, he spat, that's a lie, propaganda. The butterflies descended on their group, slaughtering them one by one. He saw them skinning his friends and eating the rest, everything soft and gooey, all the bones and meat, and from the skin they made the costumes to wear when going down the mountain among the people. The werewolf from the story was the reason he survived. Before the butterflies did that to him, the lone wolf found him. He saved him and kept him safe from the butterflies. The werewolf showed him how to kill them. How to hunt for food. How to survive the mountain. How to become a wolf. He taught me all of that too. It's not only mud stuck under my claws. When I run, I feel the rocks under my limbs and the wind in my fur. He taught me how to blend in with the beast within, who sees only crimson and tastes only iron.

Where is that old wolf now? Silva had asked him. That's the one question he didn't answer. He fell silent, and in that lack of sound, the answer was clear to us, without a word spoken.

Since I started writing his story, I should finish it. I asked him once if he's going to show me the grave of his savior, the one who made him like this. I don't know why I asked that. What I planned to accomplish. He started laughing at that, forceful, almost choking on his own spit. Didn't I already teach you that we don't waste anything up on the mountain? I think that was what he said. Or something along those lines. His agony was the only human thing left in him, and at that moment, it was hard to remember that it had been a very long time since he'd been human. If there's anything that I should remember, it's that his first gift to me was the pain.

Remember—loneliness is heavy. It's worse than drowning. I exploited his loneliness to make him go against his wishes. I begged him to return to the others in the camp. Said that the wolves aren't meant to be in pairs, but in packs. I think I said something stupidly corny like that. I promised that everything would be better when there's more of us together. That it's easier in a bigger group. I was ready to say anything, just for him to let me go from his den.

Remember—it's strange that he can even converse with us. He's illiterate, never learned how to read, but he speaks an almost perfect contemporary Croatian. Almost. He has his mistakes. That's how I know that our communication isn't the work of some kind of magic, because if this world is all twisted, why wouldn't the wolf speak in his tongue, and I hear him in mine? No, sometimes he says something, a word or a phrase, sounding like it came straight from some old book that had been assigned reading in school. Similar to those ~~people~~ monsters from the village. The implication being that he somehow manages to follow the changes in the language, through the years, which isn't a thought I like to delve on too long.

Remember—donkey legs taste like cold pork. The texture of fur on the tongue is horrible. But I ate with gusto. Marina too. The grease from the skewered meat dripped on her chin, while she ate over the fire in our improvised camp. She ripped big chunks of meat with her teeth and chewed loudly. The pure, unbridled rage burned in her eyes. She tied her hair in the green headscarf. A trophy, she told me, that's what it was. Marina would've been the perfect wolf.

Remember—Silva disappeared just like Slobodan. During the night. We hadn't been sharing a tent, due to the obvious reason. The only thing we need is a shelter made out of branches. Marina and Lori didn't hear anything through the whole night. The wolf also said he'd blissfully slept. I know he's lying. I know that, at some point during the night, he went somewhere and how long it took for him to get back. I can't challenge him because I know, if it had been him, I would've heard the struggle and the fight. I know I would've heard the slaughter. The placement of the ritual stones. The removal of the tent and all her things. But I didn't hear any of these things. The only thing I could hear was Velebit's nightly song I've learned how to ignore. The next night, though, I could swear I could hear Silva's voice among the invisible singers. I can still hear her singing in the choir of cursed souls before I fall asleep.

Remember~~—skin is warm under my touch, and fur is soft.~~ He's covered in a network of scars, hiding hundreds of stories Silva will now never be able to collect and document. Sometimes, I imagine he has no skeleton. That he's missing the organs and tendons. That he's only filled with blood. I imagine him like a wine pouch, for me to tear open and drink the sweet alcohol up. Regardless, he has teeth, sharp enough to rip out wings. Marina had told me not to be stupid. Not to make a horrible situation into an even worse one. Since we're stuck in a horror movie, I should at least accept that some monsters can be on our side, rather than against us. Even if that means for me to **[The next word Hrvoje crossed out so much he almost broke through the paper. Unlike the other strikethrough segments, it's impossible to read what he originally wrote here.]** make him trust me that I'm never, ever, going to leave him all alone.

Remember—I watched Marina kill the snake with a rock, smashing her small horned head with one precise hit, while I sat at the side, uselessly keeping watch. She didn't stop there, and with forceful punches, she mushed the snake into minced meat. Lori had given the snake a name. Her breasts were covered in tiny puncture wounds, bulging from the swelling, and her nipples were half eaten, leaking pus. She had given the snake a name and cooed like it was a baby. Marina's hits left wet splashes ringing in my head while the rock rose and fell in an arch, splattering blood drops in the air, all over Marina and the moss.

Remember—when Lori asked me, I claimed I saw the snake slithering inside the mountain's rocky hole. Lori didn't believe me. She didn't trust Marina when she said the same thing. Her cries that night were louder than the wailing of the dead souls.

Remember—I managed to keep my mind mostly thanks to Marina. Out of us all, she maintained the best connection to our old life. The most rational one, someone would say. Focused on getting us back. She rewatched the video footage, analyzed it, and believed she'd figured things out. The camera shows us the truth, even if it's distorted. It's still better than our eyes. Everything went to hell when Lori walked through the Turkish Door pass. Lori somehow unlocked the door. Maybe she could unlock them in the other way too. We just need to find our way to them.

Remember—Lori didn't look angry while she called out Marina's betrayal. Only disappointed. As if she expected better from her. Marina begged Lori through her tears to wake up and accept the truth. To see her bitten breasts leaking yellow mucus from the open wounds. I think I'll never forget Lorena's cackle at that moment. I don't want to remember it. That can stay locked in my brain with some other things I've buried deep inside, not wanting to touch them with a pole. Lorena said, in the end, that she sees the truth clearly now, that she should've listened to some old baba before, when this baba had called to her. That she shouldn't have stayed with us. With Marina. I admit, that landed on Marina like a slap. ~~Do I have to remember how Lori raised her hands to her head, put each palm on one ear and pulled, tearing the skin away before our eyes? I don't want to remember the sounds of the skin breaking at the seams. I don't want I don't want I don't want to remember the pink tissue nor the eye sockets nor the way~~

~~she threw her skin away, on the sharp rocks, like dirty underwear, and spread her wings, turning her back to Marina's furious scream.~~

Remember—that happy sensation when you sunbathe. Remember the sun. The sun should be somewhere behind the clouds. That was probably what Marina wanted you to remember.

Remember—there's no sheep on Velebit. Only butterflies, snakes, and wolves. You're either with one or the other. Lorena left her skin and a desperate Marina. The grief hollowed her out from the inside, pierced her like a balloon. In my pocket, I have a piece of Lorena's skin. **[To preempt the question—no, the police didn't find Lorena's skin in Hrvoje's pockets. They did find foreign tissue matter under his nails, but the DNA isn't a match to anyone in the group, but probably from his attacker, whom he'd scratched in the fight, which is consistent with other defensive wounds. Unfortunately, the DNA sample of his attacker is contaminated because the analysis shows, at the same time, it's both human and animal.]** Just a miniscule, rubbery piece I tore from the rest with my claws. I'm not even sure which part of her body it used to cover. I'm not sure, but if Lori was a key, maybe only one cut will prove to be enough to find the lock. Worst case, one can force his way through locked doors. You just need to find them.

Remember—the camera is perfect for that. Sometimes, I rewatch the old footage, and memories jolt my brain awake, pulling the wool away. There's life, my life, on the other side of the mountain. That's probably what Marina wanted me to remember. I'm sure of that. I just wish I could talk with her. I miss her. I don't want to remember what happened to her, but it keeps nudging at me. As if she doesn't want to be forgotten. A horned viper. Of all things. Of all the fucking things. After tearing out huge butterfly wings with her own bare hands, after she bashed a named snake with a rock, in turn, a nameless one got to her head. Marina sat down on the pile of rocks without checking it. A swift head struck out from a hole and bit her. Everything happened so fast I couldn't even get to say thank you. For what? For everything. ~~You don't waste anything on the mountain so a part of her will always stay with me.~~

Remember—Saša. Saša waits for me at home. Saša isn't filled with a red rage, burning and devouring everything before him like a wildfire. Saša's love is like the sun peeking after the rain, like a glass of cold water in the midst of the summer heat, like a warm stove during the worst winter storms. Remember that. How it feels to be loved and to love. How there's nothing rotten in that feeling. How there's no violence.

Remember—my name is Hrvoje, my name is Hrvoje, and I'm not of this mountain. I have parents and an older sister who must be worried sick. I have a partner who waits for me. This mountain is not my home. It never was. It'll never be. I need to find the door. I think I'm close, I must not forget. I need to be very careful so he doesn't figure out what I'm planning. Otherwise, it'll end in blood. He will not want to let me go, but my teeth are now ready. I'm not clawless anymore, not without my own set of sharp canines, as I was when he found me, ~~all thanks to him~~.

I will not let him get in the way between me and the door, even if I died in the attempt. I just need to remember that, under the wolf pelt, I'm still just Hrvoje, Hrvoje who wants to go home. I need to remember.

Remember—

[The entry cuts off.]

22. The email I found by accident while I was collecting the correspondence between Lorena, Silva and Hrvoje to include in this booklet. This piece of the information has obviously never been leaked to the public, because nobody knew about this before. It was an email sent from Marina to Hrvoje, while they were in Jablanac, the night before their ascent to the Turkish Door, but it was sitting unread in the spam folder until I found it there,

searching through Hrvoje's emails. I thought very hard and long whether to include this or not, knowing this could stoke some fires, but since everything regarding the group's disappearance on Velebit is bizarre and hallucinatory, I decided to keep it. As I said before, it's up to you to come to your own conclusions.

With this email, I'm concluding the overview of the material of the lost Velebit treasure hunters.

From: Marina Kružić <m.kruzic89@outlook.com> 21. 6. 2024. 20:43
To: Hrvoje Beg (gmail.com)
Fw: your vacations in Stinica

Hrvoje, I'm forwarding this email to you, because, to be honest, I have no idea what to think about this, and it's not like I can say anything in front of the others. If I drag you to the side to speak in private, Lori would immediately notice that something's wrong. I could still do that. After reading this, if you find a convenient moment to speak with me, I would like to hear your opinion. I think I'm going crazy. I'm on the verge of canceling this trip, but we've all already spent so much money and time planning it, I would be sorry to mess with your plans just because I started arguing with Lorena that it's not smart for her to go up on Velebit. I don't actually want to open up her old wounds, and she's so happy about the hike, I don't want my decision to be the reason to destroy it all.

I'm sure you're going to tell me to just talk with her. Maybe I'll do that. When we're alone, at home. I'll see, I need to think about it. If I told her now, she could get really mad when she hears what I've done and I don't want to sour this trip with our fight.

So I'm forwarding to you the email from Lorena's sister. I contacted her on a hunch, I don't know if you're aware that we've not kept in touch as much since she's moved to Ireland. But I was bothered by Lorena's increasingly worse night terrors and since so much of her dreams are focused on her vacation in Stinica, I wanted to check if there's something missing from the story. If her sister has some idea why that would be. Something that could help Lorena. And now when I have my answer I have no idea what to do. Please, what do you think?

From: Tea Matic Moore <teaikolaci@hotmail.com> 21. 6. 2024. 13:28
To: Marina Kružić (outlook.com)
Re: your vacations in Stinica

Hi, Marina!

Thank you for contacting me. I had no idea Lorena's state had worsened, of course she didn't mention anything to me. Why would she say to her sister that she's struggling so much? She always tried to protect me because I was younger, but sometimes, I can't help but think she still views me as a child and treats me like one.

Before I say what you want to hear, if you want my opinion—DON'T LET HER TO GO ON VELEBIT, DON'T GO TO JABLANAC OR STINICA. Go to some island you haven't visited before. Or to the south. I'm watching all of your videos, I know that there's a lot of interesting places in Croatia you still didn't get to cover, there's really no need to go to that cursed place. I can't believe that she wants to go back there after everything, or that she didn't tell you what happened. But why am I surprised? Honestly, I should have expected her to return, sooner or later, and I should've been surprised, instead, that it hadn't already happened. But I really believed she'd moved on, leaving it all behind.

I should stop stalling and tell you what you're actually interested in hearing, and that would be our last vacation in the Stinica camp. Even though I was a kid, the memory is engraved in my brain, so there's no way I'm forgetting it, ever. If you want to check the details, you can always ask our mom, but I need to warn you to be very, very careful how to approach her with the questions, because that summer is, even after all this time, a sore spot for her.

We were supposed to spend two weeks in the camp, as was usual for our vacations. But then, something happened in July of 2005. We hadn't even been in Stinica a full week when Lorena suddenly disappeared. Thirty minutes—that was how much time had to pass for our mom to figure out she can't see her swimming in the sea, that she can't find her anywhere in the camp. She sounded the alarm immediately, and I remember, at the beginning, people acting like she was blowing things out of proportion, but the longer Lorena was not showing up, the more the atmosphere changed to nervous tension. I can still remember that gripping fear as if it was yesterday. Mom was mad with worry, we had to wait for the police to come for hours, and by then, almost all of the tourists in the camp were alert and had joined in our efforts to find Lorena. It had been a real nightmare, for both mom and me.

She was missing for four days. By then, the search had spread up the mountain, across the national park. Mom had attempted to shield me from the stories, but nevertheless, I heard people muttering that a pervert had probably kidnapped her and had already spirited her to the other side of the border, or that she's hidden in some basement, missing her organs, or that we'll find her raped and thrown away behind some bush. I don't need to tell you, but even now, when I remember all that, I start shaking uncontrollably. Poor mom, she had it worse. At least, I was protected by my child's brain which soaked this in almost unconsciously, but I don't even want to imagine the type of hell her mind conjured.

Luckily, all those bad predictions didn't become reality when, on the evening of the fourth day, the rescue search found Lorena wandering, lost above Jablanac, on some rocky trail overgrown with thorny underbrush. She couldn't explain how she'd ended up there. She was somewhere on the mountain, on a steep path, without food or water, dirty from sweat and dried blood, covered in scratches from thorns and sharp rocks. But besides that, she wasn't hurt. Nobody had touched her, so all of the worst theories could be laid to rest. Of course, it was a mystery how she'd found herself in the middle of nowhere, and managed to survive four days with no food and water. But she wasn't helpful in getting us an explanation. She couldn't say a lot, no matter how much and how long people questioned her. The answers she gave back were confusing, as if the time she was lost on the mountain had scrambled her brain. Which was exactly what everyone believed had to have happened.

Still, there's one piece of the puzzle on which Lorena and the police could agree. She said that, in the camp, she had met some old woman who told her a story about Velebit's hidden treasure, promising her that she could show it to her. Lorena went with the old woman, because the woman assured her the treasure was near and that they'd return right away. After that, she could only remember the hike and the forest. Why were all of us so worried? She was only gone for a few minutes? I can remember her words clearly. I can still hear her confused young voice. She had no idea she had lost four days. She couldn't explain what had happened to the old woman. But the police believe that at least that part of the story was correct. Some stranger lured Lorena away using her frail old age. Why, they couldn't speculate, and I don't need to list all the possibilities again. One of the theories they did share with my mom was that the woman probably had dementia and didn't know what she was doing; there's a chance she believed that Lorena was her granddaughter so that's why she'd picked her up. In all probability, the old woman also got lost on the mountain, a dangerous place for healthy young people, let alone the elderly. The police and the mountain rescue continued the search for the old woman, combing through Northern Velebit, but they didn't find any trace of her.

Sometimes, I wonder whether the thing about dementia was told to our mom to calm her down. Out of all horrifying reasons one could have to kidnap a kid, that sounded like the most painless. See, it wasn't done out of malicious intent, not out of sexual violence, just some poor old woman whose mind had divorced her long ago, and who saw some other girl in Lorena. It was a mistake, nothing else.

I don't know if I believe that story, but mom found comfort in those words, so I never wanted to shatter her peace by digging into the mystery of Lorena's disappearance. Instead of that, I accepted the good news offered to us, just like mom did.

Though, if I'm going to be honest, and I should, the story didn't have a happy ending right away.

I don't know how to explain this. I'm going to confess something that I've only told my husband, but no one else, not mom, and especially not Lorena. But in that moment, when she reappeared, when mom ran to her and hugged her firmly through happy tears, I was so afraid I almost pissed myself. I remember that clearly. I remember, because never in my life, not before, and not later, have I felt the absolute mind-shattering fear, just by looking at my sister. She was dirty, yes, she had dried scarlet drops around her ears and neck, but none of that caused the chills embracing me, as if I'd jumped, legs first, in the freezing sea. I didn't want to come closer to Lorena, my legs refusing to move an inch, the hairs on my neck rising. I remember exactly how I was stuck between the wish to run away and to become invisible. Just the thought I should hug my sister made me so sick I vomited right there and then, all over my feet, in front of everyone. They thought it was a culmination of tension and fear for Lorena. Nobody blamed me. I was just a child. But I couldn't forgive myself. I couldn't believe that was my first, instinctive reaction at my sister's return.

The fear subsided, of course, especially when Lorena hugged me. My body obviously let all the tension out when there was no immediate danger coming from my own sister. After that, I felt only remorse. That's why I'm telling you all this. Because that reaction still bothered me, even after so much time, but I don't want to talk about that with our mom, much less with Lorena. I do feel a bit better now, after writing this. I really hope you won't have a horrible opinion of me.

In any case, let's get back to the important part. When Lorena returned, she only had one wish, and our dear mom hurried to obey, and she would've done the same without being asked. Lorena wanted to go home. So we packed our things and went back. Still, the story doesn't end here. Because, Lorena continued asking for home. All the time. We would eat dinner and Lorena would stop and ask if she could go home now. Or we would watch TV and Lorena would turn to me and say, all of this is terribly interesting, but I want to go back home. Or something along those lines. Mom and I would always have the same response: we are back home. After that, she would fall silent, and turn away from us, somewhat sad. And then, one night, a month after her disappearance, she opened the window and stood up on the windowsill. That's how I found her. Our apartment had been on the sixth floor, and she was perching upon the windowsill, looking at the night sky. The second time in my life I freaked out to death. I thought she would jump. She turned her head in my direction, and said to me, "don't worry, I want to fly for just a moment." Luckily, mom came into the room, saw what was happening, jumped and caught Lorena by the hand, dragging her back from the window.

I don't need to mention that, after that, Lorena was enrolled into therapy, and that mom sold the apartment, moving us to a one-storey house. She was seeing the therapist for years. It was the trauma, that's what they told us. There's something hidden in her mind that she's fighting against, something her young mind can't process in a healthy way. And with time and a lot of work, she got better, stopped asking to go home, never pulled a stunt like that night with the window, but it was then the nightmares started. She wouldn't tell us what she dreamt about, she would only wake up screaming. But, other than the nightmares, she was good. She was like old Lorena again, as if she'd never disappeared on the mountain. And for mom and me, that was the most important thing. What was an occasional bad dream compared to the alternatives?

Of course, we never went back to the Stinica camp. Mom even avoided driving the magistrala road, passing Velebit and the camp. All of our vacations were moved to Istra and the island of Krk.

I honestly believed she told you all that? That you're familiar with her history, I mean, it's a pretty big thing. I think it's not okay that I'm the one telling you this instead of her, but I truly think it's better for you to know this, no matter her reasons for hiding this. I believe enough years have passed that this trip shouldn't present new problems, but you never know. Old trauma could flare up again, and who knows how it would manifest now. Or, maybe, I'm wrong. Maybe it'll be better for her to confront her past. To unlock whatever it was there in her mind that she'd locked all those years ago. Maybe that was the only path for her to truly heal.

If you decide to continue with your hike on Velebit, I hope everything will go well. I wish you a safe and happy return.

Good luck, take care, and who knows, maybe we'll see each other soon. I was thinking we should come to Croatia on our vacation. It has been too long since I saw mom and Lorena in person, I would really like it if we could all get together for the family gathering. I miss you guys!

All the best,
Tea

Other Tales of
Folk Terrors

What Lies Tangled in the River Grass

A YOUNG SHEPHERD STUMBLED upon her first change, while her bones were breaking, skin ripping at the seams and slipping from the rearranged, wet meat—until the only thing that was left of her old self was the pelt, pooled beneath her brand new human legs. She was confused and disoriented, in a strange body on a strange-smelling land. So dazed, she was completely unaware that there was someone following her steps in the midst of the thick fir forest. Only later would she learn about her mistake—after the shepherd stole her old skin from its hiding place in the hollow trunk of an ancient chestnut tree.

He'd recognized her kind from the old stories, knowing that stealing her pelt would make her marry him. How could she not? While he held her wolf skin hidden, she would do whatever he wanted her to. Become a beautiful bride, whelp him a whole pack.

Except, the tales sometimes lie and sometimes twist the truths. There may have been she-wolves like her who did exactly what the stories said. That wasn't her wish, nor plan.

Instead of getting a bride, he got an ax to his head. And when she found her hidden skin, she put it on again, opened her jaws, and swallowed him whole. There was not a morsel of the young shepherd left.

Her hunger didn't stop there. She gobbled up his herd, stole his possessions, and disappeared before any other villagers could learn what she had done. She stayed always on the move, traveling, stealing, eating, and living for centuries, her pelt kept close by and hidden, so no one could try to steal her life again.

The loud susurration was a constant noise, a soundtrack of her current life, just one in the line of the many she'd already lived, and hopefully not the last. The water had welcomed her with loud greetings when she came to tour the abandoned mill with the real estate agent in tow. It never stopped babbling while she cleaned up the cobwebs, trashed the old, moth-eaten furniture and replaced the derelict mechanisms with new technology. It hid the scraping sounds when she dragged the heavy, locked chest containing her pelt under the bed. The river had kept drowning out the buzzing of tourists, sitting on a small rickety terrace of her cafe, above the rushing water.

She found it completely maddening, her ears constantly ringing in the rhythm of the river.

But it was a great place to settle at, after a few unfortunate incidents in bigger cities. This village was split into two worlds: one of modern houses set atop a hill, and the other of a picturesque tourist trap, hidden from view of the road in the canyon. It used to be a corn mill complex, built on the fast waterfalls in the deciduous forest, but now, when people used only store-bought flour from big factories, it had to be transformed to continue living. Inside of the dead mills, a series of hotels, restaurants, cafes, ethnological museums and souvenir gift shops grew out, filling out the wooden carcasses like tumors. Some of the buildings still produced flour, but it was mostly sold as a costly gimmick for the tourists looking for eco-friendly food.

Iskra—for this was the new name she chose for herself—also sold her own flour, as well as homemade jams, but it wasn't as profitable as the coffee business. She held the best position on the waterfalls, with a terrace set on two huge boulders, rooted at the bottom of the river. Her rustic building was on the front line next to the river, which meant a beautiful view of the clear green water and other old mills towering over it. The whole place had the look of a town ripped out from the pages of a fairy tale book filled with blood, cannibalism, and children getting lost in the woods.

Iskra didn't care for the view, but she did care a great deal for the tourists. They were the easiest prey one could hope for. And since she didn't rent out the rooms, she didn't have to worry about anyone connecting a missing person or two to her. Her hunger was much easier to handle these days. She wasn't a young wolf anymore, one who craved to eat every day; whole herds of sheep or a small village to fill her bottomless belly. Only here and there through the year, to sate her need for sweet-smelling human meat when she got tired of eating lamb, pork, chicken, and veal.

Unfortunately, life put a wrench in her otherwise foolproof plan. A pandemic, of all things, in this digital future of the 21st century. This new virus, easily transmitted, put a stop to everything, especially tourism, locking everyone in their houses. Leaving the hotels as empty gaping holes, like her stomach which started to beg for a new hunt.

But the only prey there was were the other villagers and it was never a smart idea to eat your neighbors. Especially when there weren't that many of them.

A sound tenet to live by, but obviously not everyone thought like her. In the dead of a silent spring, a tragedy shocked their little corn mill village. It would appear that one day, while strolling along the canyon, a young man calmly walked into the river. He didn't react to the calls of his companion, his younger brother, but continued going further and further until he dived in, never resurfacing. The boy insisted there had been a beautiful green woman in the river, calling to them, saying something he couldn't understand. His brother obviously could, because he went after her. When he dived in the water, the woman disappeared too.

Iskra joined in the organized search of the canyon, not wanting to stick out even more than she already did. Both as a newcomer, where everyone knew each other's families for generations, and a lonely woman in her forties with no partner or children to call her own. There were some in the gathering who were obviously skeptical of the boy's recollection of events.

Others suggested that maybe there had been a drowning woman in the water, and the man had jumped in to save her, only to be swept by the rushing tide. A few looked toward Iskra, their eyes squinting with obvious distrust, probably wondering if she could be this siren who'd bewitched their youth.

She was the only one who'd understood the child and knew that the search was futile. The man was already a part of the drowned kingdom, a servant to its master, the hungry river spirit.

It was just her luck that she would manage to set up shop in the literal backyard of another hunter. One who doesn't care whether it would draw some unwanted attention or not. The frustration ran deep in her bones but she wasn't ready to move yet again. Besides, water spirits lived in the water, and she had a whole forest for herself.

There should be a way for them to peacefully coexist, surely. Thinking back on the stories, to placate the spirits, each Sunday she poured down a bit of the cheap beer from her terrace into the river, hoping it would be enough.

The spirits never answered, though, and the long nights started to get shorter with each passing day.

Spring changed to summer and with the scorching hot weather and shorter clothes came the loosening of the lockdown measures. Tourism was, for the otherwise wilting Croatian economy, a lifeline. Pandemic or not, the numbers had to be good and people had to be encouraged to travel, to come visit the Adriatic sea.

Regardless of summer, the temperature in the village was always cool, and while most people preferred to spend their vacations on crowded beaches of the Croatian coast and islands, there were those who were searching for a quieter place, away from the suffocating heat and deep in the shade of trees. People like hikers and cyclists trickled down to their mills, finally giving Iskra a chance for a hunt. During the day, she worked the tables of her café, a fixed smile stretching the muscles in her cheeks almost to the point of pain.

At night she prowled the forest, hiding in the undergrowth, touching the mud with her paws. Her hunger deepened, her belly unsatisfied with a diet of animals bred in factories and slaughtered with faceless machines.

When she found the perfect prey—a lonely hiker who didn't quite fit in his group—she didn't dally.

It wasn't hard to isolate him from the others, he did so himself, straying from the path. He was playing at the lone wolf, which suited her just fine. The sunlight was getting dimmer, rays playing with color, changing shades from light green to deep rich darks. The air smelled of moisture, lichen and moss, but mostly of sweet blood pumping through the veins of her lumbering prey. Each step he took—smashing through the broken birches, squashing crawling centipedes, staggering through the thorny bushes—left an easy trail to follow even by sight. In contrast, her great paws made no sound, as gentle as an oak's shadow cast by a setting sun. Only by design would she slip a small noise—a calculated movement here and there, the brushing of the tail, scratching with the claws, a subtle, quiet growl. Each time he would jump slightly or turn around, aware of the creeping twilight, of the forest closing in on his surroundings. His steps grew faster, more frantic, searching for a clearing, an exit, unknowingly going further and further from the village and the safety of his group.

She could've jumped at him at any time, but savored the scent of fear permeating the air. Her mouth was salivating over the promised dinner running through the forest like a headless chicken. He managed to break out of the woods, darting between the unmovable trees toward the sound of buzzing water. It wouldn't help him much, since it was too far away from the laughing people, dining at the mills.

It's time to bring this to an end. Her belly grumbled in excitement as she slipped from the trees. Thick saliva collected on her tongue. Any time now he would turn around and see her in all her glory. The canines glistening in the dusk, the lean body, the muscled legs.

His fear would then bloom fully, marinating his meat to a rich aftertaste.

Except, he didn't turn. He didn't even try to glimpse at his pursuer. His back was ramrod straight, his head facing the water.

The rushing, gurgling streamflow. And there, in the midst of the murmuration, she heard a purr, so subtle she almost missed it. Until it broke through her hungry mind, making her ears twitch. He wasn't running away from her. He was running to something else.

Her paws stopped, frozen. He was approaching a thick coat of freshwater algae—bright green, gleaming on the surface. His legs were grabbing through the water, the strong torrent barreling into his body, trying to force him down. He was already knee deep, and the green cover expanded like spilled paint, drawing closer to him.

The quiet sound overrun by the water noise grew louder now, turning into a sweet song. The words were gibberish, but meaning washed over her all the same. The severe sense of loneliness was wedged into the melody, of time lost to the ravenous melancholy. All of the years she'd lived through suddenly bubbled up to the surface. Seasons changing, people growing old, dying, the world forgetting about creatures like her. In that constant permutation, she was a fixed point. An old wolf prowling the forest, packless, simply going through new homes, new names, new lives. Never quite fitting in.

The melody changed then into a comforting touch on the arm, into a warm hug; like a teasing kiss on the lips and a body snuggled close under a starry sky. It promised days filled with soothing calm, rather than restless emptiness. When was the last time she talked to someone, not just pleasantries with her customers but an honest conversation? When was the last time she shared her bed with other monstrous women who sometimes crossed her path? If she would only follow the song, a few more steps, it would all be so much better. There was companionship in this world for everyone.

The worst thing for a wolf was to be alone in the world.

The cold water licked at her paws, breaking through the mesmerizing promises. She was walking toward the song, the river, as mindlessly as her prey before her. He was already so deep, his torso submerged, with slimy chunks of underwater grass spawning from the algae, catching him in a web of leaves. Leaving the green smudges all over his head and exposed neck. *Oh no, you won't!* She growled, her hunger exploding in anger. *He's mine, I saw him first!* Her voice erupted in a warning snarl before she took a big leap in the river, without much thought or care.

It was her dinner getting stolen, swallowed before her very eyes. Her strong body struck the water in the middle of the pulsing algae, the slippery mess immediately tangling in her fur. But her jaws caught on the man's arm and gripped hard, even when the slime got through to her eyes, nostrils and mouth. The force of her body made them dive in the green-filled current. But instead of getting lost in the stream, the grass gripped them in its strings, chaining them in place.

Blood sipped through the man's skin where she'd bitten him, clouding her vision even more. Everything was dirty green and watered-down red, slime crawling with the grass along her body, like tickling fingers. She held on to the man who didn't even try to struggle, his frame limp in her grasp. His body jerked unnaturally, like someone was pulling on him, while the grass at her limbs coiled, drawing her in the other direction. She twitched, but there was not much she could do, as tangled in the underwater foliage, not while she was latched onto someone else. Her lungs burned with lack of air, but she still didn't budge. Instead, she bit down harder, breaking the bone under her sharp teeth.

A snap, a hand dislodging from the rest of the body, ripped out with a forceful pull. Her head jerked in a sudden lurch, the piece of meat securely in her mouth. Algae and grass rushed in to fill the space, engulfing the figure of the man. The grass was still keeping her in place, anchoring her to the river floor. Her lungs and mind screamed, one for oxygen, the other out of rage.

She was stuck, drowning, her dinner gone, left only with the sorry scrap. Like some pathetic stray.

Two twinkling dark green eyes broke through the blurry darkness, shining with their own inner light, in the midst of the floating grass. Iskra twitched in her watery chains again, a nervous, angry flutter, trying to break free. A slight touch on her belly froze her in place. The feeling of fingers caressing her tender underbelly and the unmistakable sharpness of claws slightly digging into her skin overtook her senses. It would be so easy to make one fast, clean slash, gutting her open. What would it feel like, to be aware of her intestines slipping out of her body, into the thieving water?

The fingers moved across her chest, onto her head. Scratched over the fur behind her ears. A furious moan was stripped from her, through the water and arm in her jaws she was still trying so hard to keep. Did this thing just pet her? *The nerve!* Why didn't it just kill her, putting her out of this misery?

The grass uncoiled from her limbs, the unexpected freedom getting replaced by the barbarous force of the stream. She was rushing with the river, the water shoving her in the direction it wanted to go. But out of the green grasp she was able to move at will, scraping the last of her strength to push herself out of the current. To break through the surface with her head, the disembodied limb secured, and with scorching lungs. Her paws were furiously splashing, taking big strokes towards the river bank. With a tired pull, she managed to drag herself out from the river's clutches, onto stable ground.

She spat out the arm and vomited a dirty river out of her chest, green slobs dropping heavy from her mouth. Her stomach was sick with tension, her mind swimming in anguish and humiliation. The mere idea of eating this worthless remain of her carefully prepared meal tingled nausea from deep within.

The river behind her laughed with clamoring delight.

Summer season was in full swing, the mills overripe with tourists, but she couldn't find any delight in it, her pride bruised under the heavy blow. Beneath her windows, she listened to the chatter of people all day, the laughter of children, the drunken songs from elders. The restaurants and hotels were filled to the brim with people, whole lambs roasting over open flame almost each day, turning on the rod. The air smelled of greasy coconut sunscreen mixed with dour sweat, calling to her begging belly. She ignored it all, her mind still reeling from her last attempted meal, tainted with the memory of drowning, grass, and algae. Wanting only revenge.

One evening, she closed down the café and went to her rooms, getting ready for another restless night of dreams filled with burning green orbs and exploring, cold fingers. The rotting smell of decay hit her hard as soon as she was at the door. Her eyes snapped to the source at the open window, where a bloated, one-handed corpse lingered. The water had transformed the body into a purple bladder, seeming unstable to the point she could imagine popping it with a needle, draining it of the excess liquid. It was only by the fact of the missing arm that she recognized her lonely hiker.

Iskra froze at the door, her mind completely blank, fear gripping at her throat. From his remaining arm her pelt was hung. The wolf pelt that should've been locked safe under her bed, dangling freely over the window. Towards the cascading waterfall.

Something snapped in her mind, pure instinct taking over. In haste, her human legs ran across the wooden floorboards, her arms outstretched. The corpse fell out the window, her fingers missing it for a heartbeat, her fists closing against the empty air.

The splash of the body hitting the water was loud enough to break through the constant susurration, and when she leaned over, instead of the clear water letting her glimpse at the sharp rocks, there was only a deep, mossy green welcoming her.

A scream of anguish tore out from her mouth.

"Why are you doing this to me?! You won!" Iskra's yells floated down, swamped by the gurgling. If she jumped over, she would surely break all her bones, possibly even her neck. It wasn't a big waterfall, but the water was shallow and the rocks unforgiving. But the green was waiting for her, taunting her. And what was even the point of living if she didn't have her wolf skin, to change to her true form whenever she wanted to?

Taking a deep breath, she plunged through the window, feet first, toward the water below. In free fall, a trite thought passed through her mind. Maybe the spirits didn't like the Karlovačko she spilled for the offering. Maybe she should've gone with Paulaner instead.

And it was with that thought she hit the river, feet breaking the surface. Instead of rocks, it was a mess of moving grass that caught her, curling up her legs. Stroking her thighs. Dragging her deeper into the darkness, while her brain yelled it was impossible. Surely she was dead, having broken her neck on the rocks, her battered body being dragged by the current. This was her hell, this complete emptiness, just endless water stretching before her, great big tangles of tall grass palpitating around her. Devouring her.

The pull on her legs continued, twisting her body. She lost all perception of what was up and what was down, knowing only of water in all directions. Of the touch of grass on her legs, of a slight caress at her spine, her neck, her breasts. She caught one strand in her palm, squeezed as much as she could, and pulled. Wasn't sure what it could accomplish, not when she was so thoroughly covered in them, in this body, in a stranger's territory. Regardless, she would not go down without a fight.

The grass under her armpits yanked at her, hard, her head breaking through the surface she didn't even realize was so close. She drank in the air, blinking out the water from her eyes. Tried to see where she was.

The world was dipped in a green tint. Instead of blue, the sky was painted honeydew. An enormous bulrush cluster grew from the muddy river, as big as prehistoric trees. And she wasn't alone.

Tangled in the grass were drowned corpses, floating like logs in the water, their glassy eyes turned upward, watching the sky. A small island protruded in front of her, made of slick mud, and a woman shrouded in underwater grass sat on the edge, her legs submerged in the still water. She was looking at Iskra with two twinkling green orbs for eyes.

Iskra blinked, and finally understood what she was looking at. The constantly moving underwater grass, covered in algae, so long and rich it flowed down along her body to the water, growing out in an endless stretch, was the woman's *hair.* It was everywhere in the river, an inescapable mass. It was the woman's hair that had pulled her, that had held her immovable when they'd first met. That swallowed her up when she jumped from the window.

Tangled in this squirming, grass hair were small crabs, their little pincers opening and closing in the air. On top of the woman's head lay a woven crown of water lilies and shells. At her back was the corpse that had broken into Iskra's home, stealing her pelt.

Which was currently laying in the woman's hand.

With the other she caressed it, like it was a damned coat made for her, not a piece of someone's skin. Iskra bit down on an angry reply, aware of the slight touch of grass all over her body. It wasn't holding her in a grip at the moment, but it might coil over her in a blink of an eye. She had to keep calm if she wanted to stay alive and get her pelt back.

"I see you're angry," the woman's voice was as whispery as the rush of the waterfall, as slippery as a wet rock that could bash through the skull, "I'm sorry, but I wanted to speak with you and I wasn't sure you would accept my invitation after... you know. Last time."

Iskra floated in the water, unamused. "That's mine," she growled.

The woman simply chuckled. "I know, that's the point." The grin split open wide, showing off a row of short, sharp, triangular teeth. "I didn't expect a divine she-wolf so close to me.

How exciting. Sorry for almost killing you, I thought you were just a wolf or a really big dog."

"*Vodenkinja,*" she spat out the old term like a curse. A water spirit. A river fairy. Whatever she wanted to be called. "Am I dead?" Iskra asked, her eyes glancing at the bloated corpse kneeling behind the woman, in supplication. Waiting for new orders. Unblinking, unbreathing, unfeeling.

"Why would you be dead?" She sounded genuinely confused.

"This is the realm of the drowned, is it not? Did I mistake it for something else?" With her arm she encompassed the endless water and tall bulrushes, splashing with movement.

The woman, vodenkinja, grinned. "Oh, you're not mistaken. But I haven't drowned you. My hair in your lungs helps you breathe."

Iskra blinked, her hand going to her neck instantly, feeling the skin as if she expected to find something under it, a thin blade of grass tickling down her esophagus. She was acutely aware of the grass floating around her, touching at her skin in soft caresses.

The woman's laughter rang merrily in the otherwise lifeless silence filled with cadavers. "I'm joking. Relax." Her chuckles died down under Iskra's hateful gaze. "I'm sorry, this is all going wrong. It's just that it's been so long—"

"Let's cut this short. Where's your master? What does he want?" Iskra could recognize when someone was playing with their food. She will not die in disgrace. Better they kill her now, or she'll find a way to strangle the vodenkinja with the woman's own hair.

"Master? What?" It was, strangely, the most serious thing she'd said so far. Her eyes, full of deep green light, flashed with bewilderment. "Ah, you think I sing for someone else. This is my river—" she spread her arms, indicating the world around her "—these are my servants." She pointed at the corpses floating around. "And my food, of course. I'm on my own. Why do you think I work for someone else?"

Iskra cringed. She'd made the same mistake the young shepherd did centuries ago, his head filled with folktales, believing he could tame a divine she-wolf with simple theft. What Iskra knew of water fairies was only what people used to, once upon a time, tell in hushed voices. A cautionary tale of the drowned kingdom ruled by water spirits—vodenjak and his vodenkinja who will sing a song to lure people to their watery deaths. But she was a living proof the stories get the truth wrong. Twisted.

"So why am I here?" She refused to answer, trying to avoid looking like a gullible fool.

The vodenkinja let out a deep sigh. It was so familiar, the sound itching at her own chest. "It gets lonely here," she said with a shrug. Her hand was still gripping Iskra's pelt, but at least she wasn't petting it anymore. "All my servants are so silent, speechless. My river is full of life but it's only plants and animals. I can't really talk with frogs or crabs. Well, I can, but... it's not a very fulfilling conversation. If you know what I mean."

"You stole my skin as bait, to get me here, so we could *talk*?" Iskra puffed, incredulous. It was getting cold in the river, but her anger was enough of a coat to keep her warm.

"Like I said, I wasn't sure you would come of your own volition. And I really wanted to properly introduce myself..."

"That doesn't make it better. Like, at all."

"I know, I know," the water spirit said, and her shoulders slumped. Maybe she felt ashamed. Iskra didn't care. She just wanted her skin back. "I made it all worse. First I almost ate you by accident, now this—"

"And you definitely ate *my* prey."

The vodenkinja pouted. It was such a ridiculous sight to behold, her plump lips closing over the teeth, hiding the sharp needles. She rose to her full height, which wasn't much, it would seem. Iskra couldn't be sure, but it looked as if the woman's head would only get to Iskra's shoulder. Still, her hair was more than compensating for the lack of height.

The vodenkinja went in the water with sure steps, the pelt in her arms like a sacred offering. The grass at Iskra's back gave her a slight push toward the woman, unthreatening, not intrusive, just an encouraging shove.

For a brief moment, as soon as the vodenkinja was close, Iskra wanted to jump at her throat, bite down hard on it, ripping out the tendrils and flesh, no matter her human teeth. She was angry enough to do that easily. But something stalled her—be it the wishful sigh, or the confession of loneliness, or just the lovely shade of green of the eyes—and she knew there was a part of her that wanted it too. Company. Someone who was not as short-lived as a human, who understood what lurked in the darkness of the forest or in the depths of the water. Someone who was the threat people told tales about.

Someone who could share her meal.

She was getting sentimental in her old age. Or mostly just tired of the world slipping through her grasp.

"Here, I really didn't intend on keeping it," the vodenkinja said, pushing out the pelt to the floating Iskra. Her arms snatched it in a blurry motion, even faster than her own mind to catch up to the fact that she held her skin back in her palms. The fur was soaked wet but she didn't mind. It will dry off and so will she.

"You know I should kill you for this offense," Iskra said. It wasn't a joke. The other woman nodded, gravely.

"I hope you won't try that. You're in my domain. While you're quite a remarkable wolf and an impressive woman, you wouldn't stand a chance. Not here in my river."

While it would be an easy thing to try and refute that, their last meeting was proof enough. Iskra would be foolish to try something here. Maybe if she found a way to trick her out of the water, back there in the mundane world. She could act along, play at being friendly, and once the vodenkinja was on dry land, her hair useless on ground, Iskra could strike her down with her claws. Get her revenge and fresh dinner, at the same time.

But she didn't really like fish and, mostly, she was curious. Hadn't she poured the beer in the river in hope of a possible agreement with her watery neighbors? Couldn't she try to do something a bit different?

"If you get me back unharmed and promise never to do this again, I'll forgive you," she said in the end. The vodenkinja nodded, solemnly. Her face was close, her clawed hands floating near. They were created to tear, to gut. The thought of what those fingers could do stoked a different kind of hunger. Iskra hesitated for a bit, mulling over her next words. An idea was forming in her mind. "And we could hunt together, next time." Almost shyly, like she was some young, inexperienced girl and not an old wolf, she added, "If… it's something you'd be interested in."

At that, the green eyes lit up with new strength. And the water woman grinned, showing her row of perfectly sharp teeth.

There were whispers on land of something in the water. Of shadows in the forest. Of something large bursting through the woods, on the hiking trails. Of tall underwater grass tickling at the feet of swimmers in the summer. Of nights filled with strange, delightful laughter. Of missing people, drowned people. Accidents and monsters.

Sometimes, the gossip would mention the eccentric café owner and her even stranger companion, walking together by the river, one so tall she could touch the hanging tree limbs over her head, the other short, but with bushy green hair, draped in the warm embrace of a fur coat. A real wolf pelt, worn like a jacket.

Wherever they went the dogs would whimper and cats would hiss. But for tourists that meant nothing, and the little terrace on the waterfall was always filled.

To Stop the Screaming

LAURA WAS CERTAIN THAT, during the restless night, a house centipede had crawled inside her ear on its yellowish, thin legs, burrowing through the ear canal toward her brain. The pain pulsed hot in her head and she was sure—each time that she rubbed the sensitive inside of her ear— she could feel the antennae with her fingertips. A strong urge to take tweezers and shove them into her ear to catch the offending insect was a demon tempting at the crossroads with riches and she was so, so close to obey its intrusive encouragement. Only a miniscule part of her rational brain kept her from injuring herself, pointing out there were no centipedes; the phantom sensation of hairy little legs worming inside her skull was an illusion conjured by her tiredness.

Her eyelids were perpetually closing down with the heaviness of a crashing wave, but she was unable to sleep, not at nights, when she desperately tried to get lost in the unconsciousness, and definitely not during the days. Always shuffling around a nightmare without discernible passage of time, stuck in a neverending moment looping around an unwavering constant of high-pitched screaming.

"You're doing it wrong," her mother-in-law said, venom spilling from her voice. The older woman was always saying that with the subtlety of a hammer hitting the eye. "Let me show you how—" The rest of the words were drowned out by the wails pouring directly into Laura's right ear.

The baby in her aching arms was, once again, in a screaming match with the barking dogs from the neighbor's yard. It was her daughter's favorite activity. Laura was trying to calm her, the heavy mass clinging to her chest vibrating with the bellowing of small, but strong lungs. Laura rocked her baby faster, mumbling incoherent syllables, her eyes fixed on the view of the back of the neighbor's pink house, where two small dogs were yelling their hearts out at nothing, her mother-in-law yapping in the background. Laura was faintly aware the other woman was droning on and on about Laura's newest failure, whatever that was, but she couldn't compete with the rest of the choir.

Laura's home—her mother-in-law's house, which the old woman never let her forget—stood tall on the slope of a hill, which meant it was on a higher level than their next door neighbor's, opening a view from Laura's kitchen to their backyard, vibrant with unkempt, thorny underbrush, weeds, and parasitic ivy, the pollinators buzzing and flying over wildflowers. The toy-sized dogs were hidden by the high grass, but Laura could follow the hints of their scrawny brown fur in the sea of green. And she could hear them, right under her window, just like her daughter could.

Each time her baby collapsed into exhausted sleep after hours of crying, letting Laura free to breathe in a few blissful moments of peace, the fucking mutts would start again, their angry baying waking the baby up, and Laura's torture would restart. Her teeth were on the edge of breaking. Inside her mind, an image of mangled, blood-spattered fur was slowly forming, a chilling balm to her overheating insides.

"Are you even listening to me, you brainless bitch?"

The ugly pink house was mocking her. It was a huge block of seemingly regular shapes—a cube for the body, a triangle for the roof, a square for the windows—but sometimes, when Laura blinked, just like now, right before her the edges would blur, reshaping known geometry into something she couldn't quite grasp. Rationally, she knew that the neighbor's house was a normal two-story with a pink facade—the color of open flesh—but her eyes told her brain a different truth, showing it was also a beating organ with moist, gaping lips where windows usually stood. Laura wanted to stretch out her hand and touch the rosy membrane with the tips of her fingers, to feel the texture and see if it was the same as her warm insides.

"Be careful!" her mother-in-law shouted and the baby heard it as a new challenge, raising her wails even higher, reaching new octaves. The older woman was right in front of Laura, her cloudy eyes showering her with disgust. Before Laura could reply or even take a new breath, the wiry arms detached the crying baby from Laura's chest. Only then, devoid of the trashing weight, Laura's tense arms relaxed and she became aware how, in the last couple of seconds—or minutes or hours, because time meant nothing anymore—she'd been squeezing her daughter uncomfortably hard.

"What's wrong with you?" her mother-in-law howled over the raw cries of the baby she held. "Get a grip. Do I really need to teach you everything?" Laura's baby, dressed in bright, fuchsia-colored clothes, looked like a skinless rat, face scrunched in tears, her round little cheeks flaming red, spit and snot pouring down the chin.

If Laura hated something, it was rats. And pink. She fucking hated that color, and now she couldn't escape it, not from her baby who was different shades of it, from skin to clothes, not from the view through her window.

"I can't sleep. This needs to stop," Laura replied.

"What? The teething? I told you, you should give her the—"

"The barking. If she can't sleep, I can't sleep." And so on and so forth, perpetually. Not to mention the noise pollution. "Maybe we should call the police?" From the opened kitchen windows, the air carried in the smells of lavender, the warmth of the summer sun, and the wails of untrained dogs.

"The police? Don't be ridiculous." The cataracts in her mother-in-law's eyes were trying to convey some sort of secret message to Laura, but she was too exhausted to understand it.

"Yes," Laura said. "If not the police, then I should go and talk with neighbors." Maybe, if she explained her situation, they would take pity on her and lock the dogs inside the house.

Her mother-in-law scoffed. "What will you do? Knock around on doors and beg? People are selfish, Laura, you're so gullible if you think anyone will listen to you."

She didn't need everyone in their sort-of-suburb, a municipality on the edge of town, to listen to her, even though it was correct that almost every house on this hill had a dog, or multiple dogs, most of them guardians who barked in a domino effect. But she didn't care for the others, who weren't as loud as the two right next to her home. Only one neighbor needed to hear her out. And that should be doable, surely?

If not, I could always poison the dogs, letting a bit of juicy meat covered in rat poison drop from the window. Not my fault if they're left alone in the backyard. It was a tempting idea, she couldn't deny it. However, Laura didn't have the stomach for that, nor did she want to become that kind of person. Once upon a time she had, too, wanted a dog for a pet. In her mind, though, the dog was bigger, wolflike, with jaws that could protect her from towering men with huge fists.

Her mother-in-law was allergic to dogs and anything that could bring Laura joy, and even if she could get a pet, it would be of her husband's choosing. Truthfully, he already had one, so why would he need an animal?

Laura wasn't in the mood to fight with the other woman, so she just ignored her, as was her way of dealing with unpleasant situations. But her body was thrumming with nervous energy and she couldn't stay in the suffocating house for one more second, either. "I'm still going to try," she said while putting on the worn-out sandals, purposefully not registering any of the complaints hurled her way.

If her home was stifling in the sweltering heat, the outside was outright burning; the asphalt under her shoes pulsing with hot flashes. The searing light assaulted her eyes and her vision of the empty street swam. Her pale skin, lighter still from the time she spent closed among the four walls with her little scream-machine, burned under the blazing sun, high in the clear, open sky.

Even when she put distance between herself and her child, going further away with each step, she could still hear echoing cries nestled inside her ears.

A fence of tall laurel shrubbery encircled the border of the pink house's yard. The front of the property had a tall cherry tree casting deep shade on a thick carpet of grass. Dense lavender bushes grew in the front of the house, the brilliant purple complementing the pink of the facade. The fact that this yard was so alive with flowers and colors, when all of the other gardens were scorched to dry browns, stoked the angry fires already burning inside Laura. The urgency of the heat rising from the pit of her stomach to her throat, where it collected in spikes, propelled her right to the front door, through the small cleared path in the high underbrush.

Laura knocked with closed fists, in rapid succession. The loud knocks reverbated inside the house, followed by a shuffling sound.

It was only then that panic started building inside Laura. She didn't know who to expect at the door. Even though she'd been neighbors with these people for more than a year, moving in with her husband after a hasty wedding—planned and executed in a few weeks that now felt like a forgotten dream she'd once had—she'd never met them. Nor did her husband and mother-in-law, completely uninterested in others. Startled, she realized she couldn't even say if the neighbors had lived here before her moving in, or if they'd come later—a part of her brain insisted they'd moved in only recently, but that made no sense, she would notice and remember something like that. But Laura had spent her pregnancy in a haze, and couldn't really explain what she'd been doing all that time, how she'd lived from day to day, and even more so after the birth. No matter how much she scratched at her memories, she couldn't find any trace of her next-door neighbors, at least not before the incessant crying of her baby had become worse thanks to the dogs, which had finally caught her attention.

The only thing she knew of these people was that they had two annoying dogs she could see from her kitchen window. Well, glimpse at, more than see. They were too small, and the grass was too tall.

The shuffling behind the door became louder, almost enough to drown out the ringing in her ears. What if a man like her husband opens it, large enough to fill the frame? What would she do then? Laura cursed her own recklessness.

The door opened before she could lose her courage and bolt, and the white noise in her head rose to unbearable levels. Her stomach roiled with nausea, and Laura was on the verge of puking all over her sandals, or fainting, but then her vision sharpened on the figure of a tall, slim woman on the other side, calming her instantly.

The woman watching her was younger than Laura, or maybe she was the same age, or maybe older, but looking younger, because her cheeks weren't gaunt and there were no heavy purple bags under her eyes from sleepless nights. Her hair was silky and cornfield blonde, falling long and straight over her back. She was watching Laura with a set of bright, moss-green eyes. But what caught Laura's attention was the fact the other woman wore a light, almost see-through white dress, the shapes of her panties and her nipples clearly visible in the daylight.

Laura was acutely aware of her puke-stained T-shirt and loose pants, the grease in her shoulder-length, unbrushed hair, and crusted face. She forced her eyes to catch the woman's gaze straight on, acting as if she didn't know the state she was in, or that a pink blush was blooming on her cheeks.

She hated fucking pink.

"You're shaking." The woman's full mouth was moving, her voice the honey sweet of scalding tea. For a few moments, Laura was staring dumbfoundedly, and then her brain caught up to the words spoken to her. "Are you alright?"

Laura was in fact shaking, from head to toe, but couldn't calm down, a freezing sweat breaking over her warm skin.

"Your dogs are constantly barking," she forced the words through her sand-dry throat.

"My dogs?" the young woman repeated, one of her eyebrows slightly arched. An open smile grew on her spotless face, as if she'd been told something incredibly funny. For a moment, the young woman opened her mouth as if to reply, then closed it, and waved with her hand, as if she wanted to encompass the rest of the neighborhood made up of scattered houses across the hill. "Everyone either has a tornjak, which is funny to me because they're LGDs and no one has, you know, livestock, or they have some mix of German shepherd. Including the house across the street. Mine are tiny mutts. You practically can't see them," she said in the end.

"Maybe I can't see them, but I can sure hear them." Laura bristled. "I know it's yours, because you're the closest house. Small dogs or no, they're loud and constantly barking under our window. I have a six-month-old baby. She's teething and it's already hell, but with your dogs, there's no moment of respite. They wake her up, she starts crying. Do you understand what I'm saying?" Laura took a deep breath, surprised with the words bursting through her mouth, breaking her usual silence.

The other woman shrugged, lazily. "If that's true, why don't you close your windows?"

"Because—" Laura's tongue was heavy, and each syllable was draining her energy, and she couldn't believe she needed to draw out something so obvious "—it's the summer. We need to breathe."

A part of her knew what her neighbor would answer before she even said it. "Ever heard of air conditioning?"

Laura sighed. How could she even explain to this stranger that she couldn't use the AC because her mother-in-law didn't like it, because the *artificial cold* made her ill? Laura was suddenly so ashamed, and couldn't bear the thought of voicing the truth aloud, to show how little agency she had in her life. Especially not to the woman who walked around almost *naked* and without a care in the world.

"We don't have it. Please, just, calm your dogs down. Train them or something. Or keep them in the house. *Please.* I want to sleep." Laura knew she was being pathetic, begging in her dirty clothes.

"Sure, I could do that," the woman agreed, still with the same smug smile, but despite feeling like a joke, the relief Laura felt was stronger than shame and discomfort. "But I don't think that's the real issue here." Laura's chest constricted under the direct hit of the woman's carelessly thrown words. "You said it yourself, your baby is teething. I can hear her, you know." The full lips stretched further, showing a line of white, sharp teeth and a bloodred tongue. For a split second, the tongue flickered out, sensing the air, its tip bifurcated like a snake's, but then it retreated and Laura was only left with a rising headache and confused thoughts. It happened so fast she wasn't sure she didn't imagine it. "She's so loud, that one. We also don't have a lot of peace with her constantly crying. But you don't see me at your door, asking you to shut her up. To train her." Laura's mouth was cracked soil in a drought and she tasted iron. Her sight turned rosy, covering the other woman like some filter in a photograph.

"I'm sorry," she hissed, not sorry at all, "but it would be easier to put her to sleep if your dogs weren't making so much damn noise."

The woman's sharp laugh cut Laura under her breast. "So I see. It's my fault, still." The green eyes twinkled with amusement. Laura was getting annoyed. She was here with a plea, due to a very serious situation, and the woman was making fun of her. Fuck her and fuck her small, yappy dogs.

The other woman must've seen Laura's emotions plainly painted on her face, because her smile fell off. At that moment of seriousness, she seemed much older than Laura, much more experienced.

"Look, Laura, I know it's hard, what you're going through. The depths of your exhaustion and fear and loneliness are familiar to me too." The woman's voice was soft and soothing, but somehow, that was even worse than her mocking. "It's not that I want to ridicule you. It's just that I know the help you need is not the one you're asking of me right now." She leaned over the threshold toward Laura, and a strong smell of lavender and wet ground tickled her nose. "And you know it yourself."

Laura almost barked out that the other woman didn't know a thing about her and how dare she assume, but then her brain rang the alarm bells.

"How do you know my name?" she asked, her voice the quiet squeak of a prey animal.

The woman's smile came back, but not vicious. It was kind, friendly, but also a bit sad. "You're married to an obnoxiously loud man. Unfortunately, unlike your husband or your daughter, you're very quiet, so I don't know *his* name."

Laura didn't have any spit in her mouth to swallow. Her legs were shaking and she was afraid she would lose balance and fall down in front of this woman whose words were flaying her alive.

"Just... keep your damn dogs quiet or I'll call the police!" Laura shouted, in absence of anything better to say, and started backtracking away, as fast as she could, without looking like she was running away in fear. The image of her neighbor striking like a snake, biting Laura in her neck, pumping out venom, flashed through her mind. But the tall, blonde woman didn't move from her spot at the open door, watching Laura's retreating form intently but silently, waving a goodbye at her.

What kind of woman doesn't want a child? A monster. Laura used to remember her mother's words regularly, from a random conversation they had when Laura was a teen, and recently they came back at any given time, no matter what she did. Ever since the twin lines showed up on the test, to the moment it was confirmed, to when her doctor refused the abortion invoking conscientious objection, the *monster* would swim up from her subconscious to the conscious mind and a bout of nausea would shake her insides.

Monster, monster, monster echoed even now, while she was preparing chicken for dinner, slathering a dose of oil and mixed herbs on the tender, hairless body. A bit of rosemary and parsley, a lot of Vegeta and paprika. She used the food brush to make sure it coated the whole of the body, under the legs and armpits, back and front, before sticking the pan inside the preheated oven and setting the timer. Who was she even making this for? Her husband will be late from work, again, smart enough to limit his time in a house filled with irritating cries. But he would expect his dinner, cold or hot, tasteless or horrible. Her mother-in-law was out, on her weekly hair appointment, and would also expect food when she came back. It's the least Laura could do, living in the woman's house, getting free help with childcare, as her mother-in-law pointed out, even though she hated everything Laura put on the plate. It was either oversalted, or not salty enough, burnt or too raw, too dry or too greasy, always this or that, always something wrong.

The meat sizzled slightly in the oven and Laura smiled, rocking on the soles of her feet. She hummed quietly to herself, eyes closing down. The house was peacefully quiet. If only it stayed like that. If only her husband got into a car crash on the way home, and the police had to report to his grieving widow that, unfortunately, his disembodied head had rolled out on the road where it got crushed under the tires of another car. If only the hairdresser would slip and stab her mother-in-law with scissors, slicing the jugular. Both visions were so vivid inside her mind, she almost salivated.

The image of her neighbor standing in the open doorway in her light white dress slithered in front of Laura's eyes, breaking through the violent daydreams. The woman, whose name she didn't even know, hadn't asked for, even though she knew Laura's, was covered in a red substance herself, crimson covering her long, corn-yellow hair, splatters painting abstract shapes on her face. It was the blood of Laura's husband and her mother-in-law, as if she'd walked straight through Laura's visions of carnage. Laura's guilty pleasure. The woman smiled her sharp smile, showing teeth and forked tongue, viscous drops oozing from her canines. She transformed into a snake, her scales scarlet and her eyes the green of wet moss after the rain, but Laura wasn't afraid.

Instead, she wanted to take her in her hands and cradle her to her breast. Let her bite her neck, kill her on the spot.

Laura was overheating, from the caress of the summer, from the oven, from the images in her brain. The sizzling became louder. She was not alone in getting too hot.

Shaking off the daydreams, she opened the oven, taking out the pan to turn the chicken around so it doesn't burn on one side. The pink skin had already turned light brown, getting close to golden. The meat leaked body fat and it boiled with tiny bubbles at the bottom of the pan. Laura took the spoon and started coating the meat with its own fluids. Went over the little hands and feet, tiny fingers already golden brown. The meat on the tummy was soft, and she carefully greased the skin with her spoon, so it would be easy to cut once cooked, and melt in the mouth. The face was wrinkled in a scream, or maybe a frown, blistered from the heat, eyes gelatinous bulbs bulging from the sockets. It was ugly to see, so Laura turned the chicken onto its tummy, to give the backside a chance to get the nice golden coat, so she didn't need to look at the boiled face again.

She put the chicken back in the oven and staggered. Something was wrong. She had closed her eyes only for a blink, but when she opened them, the timer showed skipped time. Only a few more minutes remained. Laura was forgetting something and it was itching her brain. Was it something her husband had asked her to do? Something her mother-in-law had said?

The potatoes were still on the counter, cleaned and cut into pieces. Oh, yes, she was supposed to add them to the pan with the chicken, but now it was too late.

I'm sure it's hard, Laura heard the syrupy voice right beside her ear. *Laura*, spoken with a velvety melody, unlike how her husband usually called her. *We hear her everyday*, and the shame swelled inside Laura's lungs again, drowning her. Who was we, anyway? The timer started coughing out the alarm, drilling away the blissful silence she hadn't heard for so long, and something finally clicked in her head. Thundering dread rocked her whole body, anxiety building in her throat like broken fragments of a mirror, slicing her trachea into ribbons. With a rising panic waking her up, drenching her in chills, she opened the door of the oven and took the pan out.

The room swayed like she was on a boat, and her sight couldn't grasp its corners. She tasted acid on her tongue and smelled the crisply cooked meat. More than anything, she wanted to scream, wanted to run away, wanted to take the knife in her hand and open her throat to get out the shards stuck there. Discarding all of that, she took two forks into her trembling hands, and tried to turn the body in the pan. It slipped a few times from the forks, too heavy, and she discarded the cutlery for her bare hands. Hot pain seared through her palms, the boiling skin and oil burning her. But she turned it on its back, to face her.

The baked chicken had arms and legs in place of drumsticks and wings, and instead of a beheaded throat, there was a head with a face and cooked eyes and a little, screaming mouth.

Laura stood there with aching palms, horror mounting from the bottom of her stomach to her brain which refused to acknowledge what she was seeing. The chicken she was supposed to cook was defrosting on top of the stove, by the potatoes. It was her baby, naked and seasoned with oil and herbs, in the pan. Maybe it was not too late, maybe she should just take the sunburn balm and spread it over her in a healthy amount, before putting gauze over the skin. The baby was only sleeping, so if Laura does that before she wakes up, maybe she will not be in too much torment. She should do that before her husband or mother-in-law came back, before they see what she's done, how badly she's fucked up. Laura couldn't move her legs, rooted to the spot in front of the oven, her eyes glued to the blisters and eyes darkened like a lamb's on a spit. They were not moving. They were not seeing. Her baby was quiet.

The sudden sharp barks from the neighbor's pink house jolted Laura from her frozen stupor at the oven, her burned palms breaking out in bright pink. The chicken in the pan was slowly cooling in the open air, and the high-pitched cries of her baby daughter signaled her waking up from her sleep, safe in her cradle.

Laura's skin was wet with sweat and her tremors were so strong she could shake the whole house. She ran toward the sink and started throwing up yellow bile, exorcizing, alongside the bitter fluids, the nightmarish image of her daughter baked for dinner.

Her husband was out again, leaving Laura with the purplish traces of his fingers on her upper arm, his hateful mother and the wailings going up and down the octave the whole day. If only Laura could, too, run away from the baby spluttering tears and spit from a frothing mouth, she would do just that. She would pack her bags, get outside the door and start walking in whichever direction, until she was so far away her ears stopped ringing.

The dogs didn't stop barking. Hyperaware of the next-door neighbors, Laura spent hours over the kitchen window, gritting her teeth and very much spying. People were coming and going from the pink house the entire morning. On the counter, there was an open notebook with shaky notes. She'd counted two men, one woman, one person whose gender she couldn't discern, to come out of the house at different times, and two different women who came to the house, none of which were the young woman with cascading golden hair she'd met. At least she was certain she saw that order of events. But when she looked at her notes, she saw, in her handwriting, written down: one man, one woman, one person—with a question mark—leading a lamb on a line, the body of which was covered with a writhing snake, squeezing it slightly while it moved. One hairless dog, foaming at the snout, walking in step with the woman who got inside the open mouth of the pulsing organ mimicking a house, wet with mucus at the pink lips of its jaw.

Laura ripped out the page from the notebook, shredding it to tiny pieces so no one could see her notes. Making sure that the *help you need is not the one you're asking* and *you know what you need* disappears in the scraps. *Come, Laura, you're welcome to join us* was the last sentence she ripped apart, but it remained seared in her mind.

She couldn't think with the barking reverberating inside her skull, not with the baby shrieking in tandem.

Laura took the sharp knife from the drawer, a chill stroking her tense body, cooling the heat that had been building up. Her daughter was crying in her cradle, but Laura was too afraid she would do something to her ever since the dream she'd had. Every time she looked at her daughter, she would see the crisp skin and gelatinous eyes, and strong disgust would shake her to her core. Her mother-in-law had to step in more and more, and there was no end to the reproach from both the older woman and Laura's husband, from their judgmental stares and vomited insults. And his bruising fists punishing her failings in motherhood, while the old woman turned her cataract-filmed eyes to the television and turned the volume up, up, always up, with the baby screaming the cherry on the top of a bitter cake.

The image of the knife she held in her palm digging inside her own stomach and splitting her up like a ripe tomato, the wound dripping with rosy juices onto the clean floor, slid in front of Laura's eyes, tantalizing.

It could've been so different, a voice whispered to her ears, almost drowned by all the noise carried in the air. She dismissed the image, turned, said something to the old woman; she wasn't entirely sure what came out of her mouth, static filling her ears with water, which distorted the words. Whatever it was, the woman let her go outside in her house slippers and dirty clothes, the blade glinting under the scorching, unforgiving sun burning her scalp.

Laura walked right into the garden smelling of lavender in the shade of an old cherry tree. The grass was cushy under her steps, the ground wet even though they were in the middle of a drought.

The garden stretched around the pink house with vegetable plots, the tall green stems filled with red bulbs. One yappy dog was in the lettuce, sniffing the leaves, as if it were searching for something.

Laura gripped the knife harder. The dog was not paying attention to her. It had brown, curly fur, and the short stubby legs of a dachshund. The fur was coarse under her fingers and the dog didn't even growl at her while she was taking it in her arms. It was so small, almost the size of her baby, docile, trusting, even of a stranger with a long sharp knife she put under its neck, its red tongue lolling from the open snout.

"You know, Laura, you could've just knocked on the door," a voice behind her back tickled her at the nape and Laura swiftly turned on her heels, the dog under one arm, and the kitchen knife in the other.

The neighbor she had met when knocking at the door was standing on the house terrace in the same, or similar, light white dress. Watching Laura intently, but without fear, leaning on the fence, above her head a crown of flowers, hanging from the pots. Laura didn't hear the opening of the terrace door, didn't hear her steps. The dog under her arm was calm, the fur scratchy.

"I..." What could she even say? The other arm, the one with the knife, shook slightly, but she hadn't drawn blood yet.

"Don't get me wrong, I'm glad you decided to accept our invitation. But most people knock at the main entrance."

"I didn't accept anything," Laura scoffed, her sweaty palm gripping the handle. The sun was shining right at her head. Salty drops fell over her forehead, nose, lips, and neck, and she could smell her own stench.

"What are you doing, then?" the other woman asked, watching Laura with an amused smile. "You know this is not what you want."

"I want to sleep." Laura's voice was laced with despair. "I want to fix... my life," she finally confessed. Why not? No one could understand. Not her family, not her Church acquaintances, because she was now certain no one was actually her friend. She didn't have those anymore, not since she'd dropped out of college to have her daughter, not since she'd cut her only friend out with surgical precision, the only one who knew how to make her laugh and fill Laura's life with joy, because she couldn't bear her own need to kiss her every time they met. She wouldn't understand, she wasn't in the Church, and Laura didn't have it in her to explain.

For a long time, Laura believed her congregation was the only community she needed, but they all preached that her whole worth was connected to her daughter and the ability to care for her, that her life should now orbit around the baby's needs and nothing else. And even if she told them the truth, how unhappy she was, how she was a captive in her own home, how she hated her husband who had started to leave marks of his displeasure, they would only judge her. She was unhappy because she wasn't a good mother, wasn't a good wife, because she was a monster. That's what they would say. That's what her mother had said when Laura had asked for advice, sobbing on the phone, at some low point a few weeks ago. *Stop being so selfish*, her mother had warned, and Laura learned to accept her new position in this world.

This woman, though, this neighbor she'd met only for a few moments, she was a stranger, not from her congregation, not a relative, and somehow, or maybe precisely because of that, Laura trusted that this woman would listen to her. Laura was holding the sharp blade for cutting vegetables at the neck of her dog, ready to butcher it, and yet the woman didn't even seem bothered, talking with Laura like it was the most normal thing in the world, to threaten other people's dogs.

The lure was always sweet to the prey, and Laura wasn't gullible enough not to recognize the siren's song for what it was, but it was prettier than the cries that waited for her when she got back to her home. From her daughter, but, also, from her own throat.

"You know this is not the answer," the woman said, her green gaze pointedly turned toward the animal in Laura's clutching arms. The spongy, wet tissue undulated under Laura's fingertips. Her head turned down to look at the dog in her embrace.

She found a naked, furless skin on an elongated, legless form like an enormous lobworm, writhing in her palm. The eyeless snout sniffed the air, showing twin fangs that couldn't fit inside the mouth. Laura jerked, repulsed, instinctively opening her arms, dropping both the clinging knife and the thing she thought was a dog, that fell on the ground with a loud splashy sound. Leaving the trail of slime on her body.

"What, what?" Her voice trembled with unsaid questions, so much shoved into one simple word. It was just like the trick with the house, the different visions she sometimes saw. It had to be from sleep deprivation. Looking at the dog-sized worm, burrowing under the lettuce, deep in the ground, she suddenly couldn't find solace in that simple explanation anymore.

"Come, and everything will be clear," the woman's sugary voice promised, right at Laura's side. The woman's delicate hand replaced the knife she had been gripping before, Laura's palm empty after she'd dropped it. How could she come to her so fast and without Laura noticing her descent from the terrace? Laura couldn't believe anything anymore. Not her sight, not the passage of time. Not even that she was alive. Maybe she had stabbed herself in the stomach and that hadn't been just an illusion conjured by her tired mind, maybe she was bleeding out on the floor, her mother-in-law eating her mushy organs, and her baby exchanging breast milk for the blood gushing from Laura's wound.

Before her eyes, the pink house shivered and gasped, transforming again into pulsing flesh, opening the lips up like a door, and Laura went in, pliable to the silky touch that led her inside.

The house was made of dreams and secret promises whispered under the blankets, just the light touch of salty air while cooling on the beach in the shade of cypress trees. Red oozed from the walls in an imitation of sweat on skin. *Is this real?* Laura asked. *Why wouldn't it be*, was the answer from multiple lips, bouncing around walls.

The other woman said to call her Kuma, and Laura wasn't sure if it was a nickname of some kind, a special title, or if her parents really did name her that. Laura almost joked about dresses and pumpkins, but her lips were glued shut together, her heart beating so forcefully she thought it would break through her ribs. There were more people in the house, just like she saw from her kitchen window, but their names and faces slipped from her mind, like a picture frame too big for a nail. She was only certain of two things—they weren't relatives or family, and they all orbited Kuma, who seemed an unofficial leader. High priestess?

A godmother, the hint was in the name, after all.

Laura took a deep, soundless breath, her eyes trying to accept opposing truths. She was sitting at the kitchen table, the smells of strong Turkish coffee permeating the air, the sugar cubes and milk near her porcelain cup. She was sitting on a breathing lung, grown from the membrane under her feet, the table a white bone from some gigantic animal, the smell of blood in the cup in front of her a strong iron. She was sitting in a ruin, on the moss-covered stone, the holes in the walls letting the sunlight in to caress her cheeks, the smells of earth tingling her nostrils.

The constant was Kuma, her long blonde hair and inviting green eyes, sitting right at her side. Everything else blended in colors and smells, in reds and greens, in mucus pinks and earthy browns. Other people mingled around them, unimportant, faces melting in the background, carrying dog-worms in their arms, forked tongues slithering in and out of their mouths.

"Are you some kind of satanist?" Laura asked, internally cringing at the question and how feeble it was. Kuma smiled her toothy smile.

"No. Our Goddess is older than your Christian god, older than his Satan. She was here long before him, even long before Slavs settled on this land."

Before the Slavs? Laura wasn't well versed in history, but she wondered if that meant Illyrian, vaguely remembering that name in the context of distant Croatian past. It was too much for her to grasp. But she didn't need to. That wasn't the important part.

"I don't know how I came to this point," Laura said, sipping black coffee just to do something with her arms, to occupy her mouth, her eyes never leaving Kuma's at the bone table. The taste on Laura's tongue was that of mud.

"It doesn't matter, it's only what you will do now that matters," Kuma replied and Laura laughed at how ridiculous that sounded. How pretend profound, a sort of wisdom one could find printed on welcome mats or mugs. It was different to one caught in a web of lies and the sacred contract signed under the watchful eyes of a serious priest and the painted fresco of the Virgin Mary with her god-child.

"I didn't want to be a pariah," Laura admitted, using an euphemism rather than slurs that surely others would use to explain her behavior. She knew she was doing this wrong, telling her story from the middle, but somehow, even with a skipped beginning, Kuma followed her without trouble. "I didn't want to be a monster."

That was why she'd let herself walk down the aisle in a white wedding dress that was too tight at her waist to the man whose shape made her physically ill. It was a consequence of a New Year's Eve party where she drank one screwdriver too many, ending the celebration in blankness, only broken in the morning when she found her naked form under the strong embrace of the friend of a friend she'd refused on multiple occasions after Sunday mass. It was her punishment for reckless behavior, for asking her doctor if he could help her, only to be reminded that what she asked for was monstrous of her, pure evil. She puked her guts out after that meeting and, knowing she couldn't handle going through the judgment again, and again, hearing the same from other doctors, she went to her mother, and admitted what had happened at the party.

A part of her had hoped for comfort. But instead, she was reminded of her responsibilities.

"You didn't want to be a monster," Kuma repeated. Laura nodded, her throat constricting. She wasn't a monster, so she'd packed all her bags and moved from the city that she loved to the isolated municipality spreading across a forested hill like a tumorous growth. And now she couldn't sleep, her baby was miserable, and Laura was an unwelcome guest in her mother-in-law's eyes. The only good thing was that her *obnoxiously loud* husband was rarely at home, and in those moments he was, she'd learned that the best thing to endure his presence was to shut down, to be on autopilot. To dissociate just like that morning on the first day of the new year of her new life. Her mind was always somewhere else. He knew how to bring her back, though, and in those loud moments of broken glasses, shouted sluts, and bruised skin, she got confronted with the truth of it all with a tight chest and tears behind her eyes.

"You don't need to be anything you don't want to be," Kuma said, leaning over the table, her long blonde hair cascading over the thin white stripes. "But you know what I think? Being a monster is not that bad." As if to highlight that, she smiled her open smile and let her forked tongue slip out, just for a second, before getting back behind pearly teeth. "Everyone is afraid of monsters. Don't you want people to be afraid of you? Rather than to do with you whatever they please. To shout at you, to hurt you, to manhandle and drag you, to fill you with unwarranted shame. Imagine if you had venom in your blood, and fangs to pump it into the bloodstream of all the priests who had imprinted their rotten commands into your skin."

Kuma's face was so close to Laura she could smell the grass and earth, the lavender and cherries. If she leaned just a bit more, their lips would connect, and Laura wasn't certain if that thought was scarier than the one where she stabbed herself in the gut, or if it filled her with sinful pleasure.

"You just need to know *who* to petition for help. Who can hear your pleas and answer them correctly. This god you currently follow is useless and uncaring, what good did he bring to you except suffering for divine purposes? And why should you?" Kuma's smile was sharp and poisonous, but it was a toxin Laura could drink any day. She was, after all, used to poison, served to her in a golden chalice, rhythmical prayers, and thin sacramental bread. This was just a different kind, and it smelled so good, tasted like unburdened freedom. "But our Mother, on the other hand... she sees you, she hears you, she cares. She helped me, you know, a long, long time ago, in a similar position. She helped all of us here. All you need is to be ready to pay the price."

That was the catch, there was always one, Laura wasn't a fool enough to believe otherwise.

Laura could try harder to be a good wife and a mother. She could maybe try to do what she didn't do before, run away and start anew. Find some other family, someone better, kinder, nicer, a safe community, that won't ask her what kind of woman didn't want to have children or get married to a man.

Her husband wouldn't let her leave in peace, she knew that. Her shame would follow, her daughter a chain connecting to him. And the courage was covered under the mountain of fatigue.

She was all alone, with Kuma the only one to offer her a chance of getting out of her misery. One that didn't end with Laura slitting her own wrists.

"I can ask for anything?"

Kuma took Laura's head in her warm palms. Laura expected her arms to be cold, like a snake, but the other woman was burning with heat as if she'd soaked all the sunlight into herself. When she kissed Laura, it was surprisingly kind. Unlike what Laura was accustomed to.

This kiss was something else. A promise. A comfort. And mostly a shot of bravery. It filled her with resolve.

"You called to our Goddess," Kuma whispered after breaking apart. "Your terrible desperation was a beacon on top of the hill and we obliged." She kissed her again, and this time it was deeper, and Laura was getting lost in the taste of the forked tongue and images flooding her mind. "You know what you need to do," Kuma whispered a moment later, her forehead resting on Laura's.

Laura hummed in acknowledgement, her sight already bathed in a sea of crimson, while the walls around them shifted from the light green of meadows to the red of external bleeding.

There was a slight touch on her arm and Laura flinched, opening her eyes. She'd fallen asleep in the darkness of the room. Standing barefoot on the cold-soaked carpet. She could hear the dripping, hitting the rhythm of a song she knew deep in her bones. Laura curiously felt devoid of fear. When she turned, Kuma was there, at her side, her long-sleeved, loose white dress clean like a wedding gown. In contrast, Laura was a study in Pointillism. She could count the drops of red drying on her face, feeling them on her cheeks and neck, following their continuous pattern down the front of her pajamas.

"How did you come in?" Laura asked, blinking fast, the vision of Kuma in her home so out of place, so sacrilegious, that she wasn't certain her brain hadn't conjured a hallucination.

"You left the door unlocked for us, remember?" Kuma's long hair was adorned with a crown constructed from twigs and lavender. Her hand was still touching Laura's and she carefully detached the knife from her slippery palm, just like a few days ago, when she'd found Laura in her garden, threatening to slaughter Kuma's dog... thing.

In the dark room, the iron smell was overpowering.

Behind Kuma, there were others, holding white candles. The flames danced on the walls, bed and carpet, sliding over the scarlet splatter.

Laura's arm hurt. Stabbing was hard when met with layers of meat, bone, and tissue. She'd made a mess. Her mother-in-law laid uncovered, the window open to let the night breeze in, the full moon visible on the dark blue sky. Now her body was cooling even without outside help. The deep gashes across her stomach, chest, neck, and face opened up her insides to inspection, and to Laura's eyes, her organs were nothing more than black smudges.

Walking in a procession, Kuma led them to the other room, where Laura's husband was strewn across in pieces, unrecognizable on their bed. His face was an empty pincushion, gunk leaking from his sockets where the knife had sliced through his eyeballs. She couldn't stop stabbing, couldn't stop slicing, getting tissue fragments on her lips, on her tongue, swallowing morsels of him by accident. The wound on his neck was so wide open, she could see the bone. The covers were soaked in red, the white walls repainted, entrails unspooled on the bed covers.

She was standing above his body, all the slimy bits and minced pieces that were left from her rage. Kuma had gone somewhere with Laura's knife, leaving her with the carnage and the candle-bearing, faceless people. She wanted to ask them if their christening had been as violent as hers. If they'd left behind a lake of blood. Someone will need to clean this up. Find every miniscule drop of the slaughtered bodies and put them in the trash. Rub the red out from the carpets and beds, cover them up on the walls with a fresh coat of paint. Will that someone be her in the end? Will these new brothers and sisters help her out? She only wanted to sleep, now that she's done her part and given her offering.

Kuma came back into the room, carrying someone against her chest with one arm, the other still holding Laura's dripping knife. A pang flared inside Laura's chest. The baby in Kuma's arms was awake and calmly babbling, as if speaking with the other woman. She wasn't crying. Her daughter trusted Kuma, more than she's ever trusted her own mother, which shouldn't surprise her, standing bathed in blood.

The memory of the night's butchery was as unreal as everything now happening in the room, like a nightmare that was skipping from one end to the other, without a coherent narrative.

Laura couldn't move from her place, glued to her spot through her husband's spilled insides. Kuma put her hand on top of her daughter's pliable head. Babies were so easy to break. Small lips smiled, showing gums and the first white-sharp tooth.

A light nod that could easily be missed under the flickering light of the candles was the only sign Laura gave. There was nothing else to be said or done. Kuma solemnly nodded back and walked over with the baby toward the bed with a sliced man sleeping atop. With a sure, quick gesture, Kuma brought down the knife, hitting flesh and bone. With a loud, wet snap she tore off a chunk of a meaty finger and dipped it into the abdomen open from the pre-existing gash, soaking the finger in a heavy coat of blood.

After a few stilted heartbeats and mushy sounds, Kuma took the finger doused in dark fluid and gave it to the baby in her arms. Laura's child hungrily took it in her chubby hands, sucking on her father's dead finger as if it were a pacifier, suckling the blood from his ruined stomach like it were milk.

Immense relief washed over Laura. Kuma's eyes became two stars on the purple-dark sky, her crown of twigs aflame like a holy halo. Under Laura's sticky feet, the ground opened, showing the vast expanse of the cosmos.

"The offering is accepted," Kuma said, her voice overlaid with hundreds of voices, with echoes of the past and the future. Laura could hear worms wriggling free from the dirt, as loud as ads blasting on a television screen. Around her, the candle flames erupted into a pyre, the shadows solemnly standing guard around her. Dozens of mouths vocalized in an eerie melody that sounded simultaneously like every song Laura had heard in her life mixed together in a maddening track, and like nothing she had ever heard before. The house centipede unspooled from Laura's skull, crawled out from her ear and disappeared before hitting the ground. The long blonde hair on Kuma's head writhed alive, growing toward the corpse on the bed, slithering over the openings in the body, the hair endings connecting like roots with the tissue inside the wide holes. The body of Laura's husband moved, rising from the blood-sodden bed, puppeteered on strings of hair. Split hairs crawled out of his broken neck and from the hollow sockets where his eyes once followed her every move and counted every breath. In Kuma's arms, the baby continued her happy suckling, her little chin stained. With big eyes, she looked at her mother, two orbs reflecting the red of fire.

Inside Laura, everything shook with the earthquake. Her stomach bloomed with petals, her lungs expanded, filling in with the cool, clean air. Her aching arms loosened, her shoulders straightened, the weight lifted. Every bone in her body shattered, the meat sliding off the skeleton like clothes that were too big. Her tongue split in the middle and the fork could sense the joy emanating from the bodies around her. On her belly, she slithered across the night sky, devouring the stars and the moon, gulping down the pure light, casting the world into primordial darkness. Her hunger was a wildfire, violent and uncontrolled, and she sucked dry the existence of her deceased mother-in-law and husband, hiding them in the pits of her stomach, as was the wish she'd asked for from her slithering Goddess.

In the background, the wordless song crescendoed in ecstasy. Laura opened her closed eyelids and found herself on her back, in the vaste of her disintegrated human body, grown anew from the steaming organs. Reborn at the mouth of the great snake, larger than the planet, her fangs bigger than mountains, dripping poison rain on Kuma's squirming live hair and the small suckling snakelet hugging her chest.

Laura woke up in her bed, mind clear and calm. Smiling, she stretched and saw it was almost noon. The house was quiet and the only thing that could be heard was the air conditioning blowing cool kisses across her naked skin. In a house that's always been hers and hers alone, people who owned it before only a bad dream in Laura's memory. As was the child that could never have happened, but who grew happily with Kuma's congregation, fed with goat blood and fresh human meat. They'd moved away from the long abandoned ruins overgrown with weeds and lavender bushes under the kitchen window of her house, but Laura will come to them when needed. Right now, the only thing for her was to relearn her new body, to sleep and rest.

The morning air and summer heat, the lavender growing from broken bricks and once-pink facade, tasted like the sweetest chocolate on her split tongue.

Notes and Reports on the Woman in White Incident

DEAR *HONORED* COUNCIL,

you'll find attached the requested documentation: scans of notes—official and unofficial—and copies of interviews and incident reports regarding the sightings of "the woman in white", outlining what was happening and actions I've undertaken to take care of it. I don't know why you're suddenly asking for these, since my predecessors never had to submit anything like it, even when they had angry mobs at the doors, but I'm only a humble servant, and it's my wish to clear the situation at my Dorm and calm your worries. I've redacted the names of the students and faculty for safety and privacy, and in their place I used their initials, as is the standard in our pedagogical documentation. I know that you don't have any experience with it, since your primary concern is the handling of Rijeka City's magical community, and not the school system, but given that my job is both, for you to understand my actions, I'm offering this explanation beforehand. Also, you'll see that I had all the reasons to take care of the chestnut tree in the garden ASAP. As for what I found... I don't know what to advise you on that particular matter, but I would like for you to think it over and see if there's a way for us to fix things, or if you just want to keep covering it up.

In case you don't think I'm able to do this job, you can kindly find another person ready to educate and make sure a bunch of hormonal magical teens don't eat their human peers, since this position is so prestigious that I'm sure there's plenty ready to replace me. But if you find my work satisfactory, I'll ask that you approve my request for an additional protection spell, if anything, this case should encourage you to update our security. I have all I need, I'm only waiting for your clearance and help.

I hope that you'll refrain from this supervision in the future, so I can do my job properly, instead of needlessly waiting for a simple decision.

Warmest regards,

Nana,

the teacher educator at the Dorm for high schoolers studying away from their homes, providing them with care, shelter, quality educational activities, and watching over the magical students for the benefit of themselves, their parents and Rijeka's magical community, as well as the safety of the human population

A scan of the note the night watchman T. D. left for the educators in our official Notebook, kept in original form with his errors with the exception of redacted names [in case you're wondering, yes, we do use a regular lined notebook as official documentation; all dorms for highschoolers in Croatia use this for the purpose of official reports that faculty members leave to each other]. The note was written during his night shift, Monday the 19th—Tuesday the 20th, November, 2012.

00:48. Disorder in the girls wing. I found [L. H.] *running in the hallway and screaming. She was obviouslly under some influence. Halucinogenic drugs probably, because I couldn't smell alchohol on her. The student was histerical and kept on saying she saw ghosts. I phoned her educator* [A. B.] *who answered on the second call.* [A. B.] *came half an hour later and took over.*

01:58. Loud speaking in rooms 115, 116, 118. I told [A. B.] *who assurred me that she will take care of it.*

The report of the interview I had with the night watchman T. D., written immediately after the fact, Tuesday, November 20th, 2012.

The incident happened during the night from Monday to Tuesday, at approximately 00:48 hours, which is when T. D. first noticed the disturbance on his cameras in the guard tower. He saw movement on the first floor on the girls' wing, of a young student he easily identified as L. H. (15), who was running toward the stairs leading to the ground level. He left his post and immediately went inside the main building, catching up to the student who was acting "hysterically", his words. Since I'm not fond of that term, I would rather note that the state he found her in was that of "heightened panic".

L. H. had been yelling, which had woken up quite a few other students who left their bedrooms to check what was happening. T. D. repeated to me that L. H. was the term I don't approve of, at which point he must've seen that I wasn't happy with him and quickly went on to clarify that she kept repeating "Help me, help me, she's following me!" (his paraphrase, to the best of his memory).

Her behavior agitated the other students, so he confined L. H. to one of the common rooms on the ground level, and ordered the others to go back to their rooms. He assumed that L. H. was either drunk or on drugs. He kept asking her what had she taken, while she was "shaking uncontrollably" and kept on repeating something about "seeing a ghost". She wanted to go home, and begged him to call her parents to come and get her, but he refused, citing that it's not his job to talk with the students' parents, which is correct. I would note here that he's not equipped nor does he have the necessary pedagogical education to work with highschool students either, which is why he called her educator, my colleague A. B., who was required to come to the Dorm right away. When A. B. came, she managed to soothe the student, and speak with the parents over the phone. After calming down, the student L. H. went back to her room to try and sleep, and the night watchman T. D. went to do a sweep of the girls' wing, to make sure that all of them are in their rooms, sleeping. He found a few rooms still awake and talking about the situation, asking him what happened to L. H. and if she'd really seen ghosts. Since those rooms were in breach of House Rules that prescribe midnight curfew, he reported them in the Notebook, after alerting A. B. that her students were "making a ruckus".

At my question whether he'd seen anything out of the ordinary, he guffawed and almost called me something unflattering to my face, but ate his words at the last moment. After clarifying that I only wanted to check whether there's a chance that another student was playing a prank on L. H., he finally admitted that no, there was nothing else he'd noticed, especially not students going around "booing under white sheets". He then asked me what my interest in this was since my group is one of the boys' and their wing was unaware of the chaos, but I managed to wave away any suspicion.

Addendum, Wednesday, November 21st, 2012: it seems that the night watchman T. D. suddenly got ill and is currently on paid sick leave. He apparently has a bad case of food poisoning.

Addendum, Monday, December 10th, 2012: At the time of talking with the night watchman I had no suspicions regarding L. H.'s "ghost" sightings and no reason to believe it was an actual Returned making an appearance (as you must know, they're not very fond of loud teens). I was expecting this to be a prank, since it is customary in our Dorm that the older students fill the heads of the first-years with the urban legend that the nuns who used to live here at the beginning of the 20th century—yes, *those* nuns, and, yes, I know we would like it if people forgot all about that, but the kids do know this building was originally a nunnery—killed people and stuffed their corpses in the walls. I didn't work directly with L. H. since she wasn't a magical student, so I had no reason to believe this was a supernatural incident.

You don't need to worry about the overlaps of this urban legend with the actual ritualistic murders that happened on these grounds. The students have no way of knowing the truth. This is a simple horror story, not terribly original, that they use to frighten young students, and which trickles down the generations.

If I started repressing it, it would only raise suspicions, which could inspire them into digging out the real past of this building and the grounds, and we don't want those bones out in the sun.

The report of the interview I had with A. B., written immediately after the fact, Wednesday, November 21st, 2012. (Note: I couldn't talk with A. B. on Tuesday during our shift, as I would've liked, because she was swamped with phone calls from parents, talks with the principal, and with the nosy students, so I only saw her in passing while she was dealing with one or the other. I also can't ask her to write up her own account because that would be so far outside of our usual job that she would surely find it supremely suspicious.)

When A. B. got a call in the middle of the night from the night watchman T. D., my colleague was, obviously, sleeping and she needed a few moments to understand what he was trying to tell her. At first it sounded like her first-year student was experiencing a particularly bad trip, which made her intensely anxious for L. H.'s wellbeing. A. B. repeatedly asked the night watchman T. D. to call an ambulance, but he ignored her, claiming it wasn't necessary, that her student was "high as balls" and that she doesn't need medical attention but a "good spanking". Instead, he said that A. B. could "bring her ass over there" and make an official decision as an educator responsible for L. H.

A. B. came to the Dorm as soon as she was able to, and found her student L. H. in the ground level common room, sobbing under the watchful eyes of T. D., who, as my colleague noted, was a "smug bastard" (direct quote). When L. H. saw my colleague, she started crying even louder, begging for her parents. A. saw that the student had soiled herself at some time during the night, something that T. D. either didn't see or which he'd ignored on purpose. She threw T. D. out of the common room, gave the girl some sugar water, and managed to get the story out of her.

The way L. H. told her story to A. was that she woke up with a full bladder and went to the bathroom. But when she got to the bathroom, she heard some sort of scratching noise in the walls and got too frightened to relieve herself. It seems that only the night before, some of the older students in L. H.'s room told her about the killer nuns and their victims in the walls. One of her roommates told her that, if she hears scratching in the walls, that means the victims are trying to claw out and that she needs to run away. At that time, L. H. didn't actually believe that the scratching came from ghosts, but the noise made her uncomfortable, so she decided to go to the bathroom on the second floor.

But in the hallway, she suddenly saw someone with long dark hair just standing there in a simple white dress. The person was standing with her back to L. H., unnaturally immobile, but L. H. thought it must be some of the older girls goofing around, breaking the House Rules. When L. H. called to her, the person in white slowly turned around, and L. H. saw that it was some young woman she had never met before, with an unnatural chalky complexion and a blank face "like a mask". The woman in white opened her mouth, but instead of sound, water trickled out, "like she took a sip of a drink but hadn't swallowed it." The water splashed over the hem of her white dress that wasn't completely white, L. H. noticed, but actually spotted with dirt as if she had been rolling on the ground outside. The woman "sort of flickered" like a flame on the breeze, and with that she seemed closer, except L. H. was at no point able to see her feet move. In fact, when she looked more intently, the woman's feet—bare and also dirty—weren't actually touching the tiled floor, instead hovering a few centimeters above the shell pattern. It was then that the woman flickered even closer to her, almost so close that L. H. could touch her if she extended her hand, which freaked her out and she instinctively screamed and turned on her heels, running away from the apparition.

A. B. told me that L. H. had kept on saying how she's "stuck in a vivid nightmare where she can't open her eyes, nothing feels real anymore, not her, not A., not the Dorm, or other students." L. H. had also admitted that she's had troubles with bad dreams before, ever since she came to the Dorm, but that she didn't tell her educator about it before, thinking she would end up looking like a child. A. assured her that it was probably just that—a dream, a nightmare fueled by the stories told by her roommates—and that she'd probably been sleepwalking.

My colleague admitted to me that she didn't believe that the girl had taken any drugs but that she had no proof she hadn't. There was a moment when she was considering calling an ambulance and letting the ER doctors figure this out, but in conversation with the parents, they decided against that, since it really seemed like a bad dream that had bled over to the waking world. L. H. managed to compose herself with the help of both A. and her parents (over the phone), and in the end, A. helped her change into clean clothes. She made the girl chamomile tea in the kitchen and let her go back to bed.

A. also briefly talked with the roommates, and asked them to keep an eye on L. H. Apparently, that night, they slept with one lamp on. A. also had to warn the three other rooms in the hallway to go back to sleep, and she came back home somewhere after 2:30. She also recapped Tuesday, her "hell of the day", since L. H.'s parents came early in the morning (they live in a small village in Lika, hours away), to take her home with them, but ended up in a meeting with the principal who insisted on them testing her for drugs in case they want L. H.'s continued stay with us. A. says that L. H. is on the first of the five years total in nursing high school, and had never before had any troubles in either her school or the Dorm. For L. H., it was "super important" for her to continue living in our city. She has no prospects at home, "in the dying village", no jobs, no schools, no ability to continue her education, and "she really wants to be a nurse and help people." A. noticed that, while the girl is not completely convinced that she'd had a vivid nightmare or been sleepwalking, she was mostly embarrassed in the morning, rather than scared, and "very adamant" that she didn't take any psychoactive substances.

The parents aren't happy with all of this, and there's even a possibility they'll take her to the other dorm for highschoolers in Rijeka. In the end, they only took her home for the rest of the week, for medical exams, just in case it was some sleepwalking situation, or maybe a mental health incident caused by her high-pressure school, and to give her a chance to calm down in the safety and familiarity of her home.

At this point, A. is mostly righteously angry at how T. D. and the principal mishandled the situation and believes L. H. was more traumatized by the night watchman's boorish behavior than any ghost she'd dreamt of. She's not certain if the girl will ever get back the trust in our Institution.

I have to agree with my colleague. Our staff, especially those who work the night shift, shouldn't jump to conclusions and should have empathy in dealing with teenagers. But that's not the Honored Council's concern, and I hope my comments on our educational system don't bore you to death. I know fully well it's not your place to interfere with the decisions of the very human principal over who works here and how, with the only exception of my placement, of course.

Addendum, Monday, December 10th, 2012: You'll notice that, at this time, there's a lack of interviews with my magical students, and you're free to think, if you want, that it's a sure failure on my part. That's because I didn't have any reason to believe my magical protegees had anything to do with this situation, so I didn't talk to them, in an official or an unofficial capacity, about this topic. I also didn't have any proof that this was really the case of the Returned, so I had dismissed this as a product of an overly imaginative mind. *See my prior addendum for explanation of the urban legend and its role among the students.*

I had also dismissed the possibility of this being a case of a mora, bringing nightmares to students while she feeds on their life energies.

While L. H. suffering from nightmares could point to it, if it were a mora, all of the incidents would've been limited to the bed, and the traces would've been much more prominent on the student. Moras aren't the most subtle creatures, and their feeding leaves the body constantly tired, empty, and bruised, something A. would've noticed. And as much as I could see, L. H. seemed healthy. The protection spell on the Dorm should shield students from creatures like the mora creeping on them, in the first place, but I couldn't be sure if it was broken or worn out. If we do what I suggested to you about updating our protective net with a new spell, I would know things like that immediately, and wouldn't need to guess whether our outdated wards work or not.

And if you're wondering, since the whole white dress thing is the elephant in the room, no, I never believed, for a second, that it could be THE woman in white. They're omens of huge turmoil, wars, plagues, and such, so why would one ever show up in our Dorm to a random student? You could argue that magical students exposing our secrets to the unsuspecting humans could be counted as turmoil, depending on the severity of the situation. Like if my štriga and krsnik student shapeshifted in front of everyone and got into an animal fight ending in busted heads, slashed throats, and ripped-out necks, traumatizing their friends and other faculty. Or maybe, I could imagine my mountain fae student controlling all of the humans in the Dorm on purpose, turning them into her own personal slaves and food source, gorging on hearts wrenched from their chests, her influence spreading over the rest of Rijeka, bathing the sea in red. My job is to prevent something like that happening in the first place, so I don't think there's anything that could happen on my watch to warrant a visit from THE woman in white, concluding it was merely A woman in white. It is a generic dress color.

Besides, I doubt THE omen of great turmoil walks around in a dirty dress.

A scan of the notes written by the night watchman M. Z. in our Notebook when working the night shift from Thursday the 22nd to Friday the 23rd, in case you're still reading this. (In case you are, which I honestly doubt, I do hope the Honored Council had asked for this amount of detailed documentation when you had my wife on your trial a few weeks back. But we both know you didn't, otherwise you wouldn't have focused on a random štriga, but found your perpetrator right away instead and not embarrass yourself. My wife says "hi", by the way, and thanks for the lovely gift you have sent to apologize—she says it's the best fertilizer for her garden.)

22:37 Room 115 is not ready for bed. Students are fully clothed and chatting.

23:01 Room 118 has lit up candles in a circle in the room. I confiscated them as a fire hazard and left them in the educator's lounge. The student [K. N.] *told me they had the candles because they were planning on summoning "the woman in white".*

23:42 Room 115 is still not ready for bed. The students are fully clothed and chatting.

00:30 On the camera feed I saw that the students from room 115 are peeking outside the room, getting slowly one by one out into the hallway, then going back inside, then out again. By the time I got to the hallway, they were all back in the room, in the beds, but wide awake and chatting excitedly. They told me they lost the bet to some other students they didn't want to name, to bait "the woman in white" to come and get them, but that she didn't show up.

A scan of the notes written by the weekend educator on duty in the Notebook, Saturday, November 24th, 2012.

At around 13:00, I found students [K. N.] *(room 118) and* [I. V.] *(room 119) drawing Satanic symbols in the bathroom on the first floor, girls' wing. When I asked them to explain themselves, they claimed that they were doing a ritual to help the tortured soul of a murder victim to find her way to the otherworld. I immediately contacted their educators and respective parents, but only managed to get into contact with* [K. N.]*'s parents. I verbally reprimanded both students for playing with Satanism, and the vandalization of bathroom walls. I also took a picture of the symbols to send them to their educators, then made both of the students clean it up with the supplies I got from our cleaner on duty, but there's still visible marks, and the walls might possibly need a new coat of paint. In that case, the damage report will have to be written and submitted for parents to reimburse the repair.*

The written report about the interview I had with my charge, the student I. V. (the mountain fairy from Velebit), written down after the fact, Monday, November 26th.

The interview was conducted as soon as I came into my Monday shift and saw the report in the Notebook left by my colleague on Saturday. [EDIT, Monday: While I. V. (16) is my responsibility in the eyes of the Honored Council as a fae, under the official rules of the Dorm, her main educator is someone else (my group is male-only students—mixed magical and human—since the rules of this Institution are heavily traditional and outdated, meaning gendered wings and groups. I work around these rules, of course, to take care of all my magical proteges, no matter which educational group they belong to. It's unnecessarily complicated, but I manage. I digress, so let's get back to the point)].

I. V.'s educator, D. J., my very human colleague, of course, has no idea that I. V. is fae folk, as is the custom, or my role for ensuring our secrecy wouldn't be needed here. I just want to note here that D. J. did her own interviews with I. V. regarding the Saturday incident, just like A. B. did with her student K. N., and both received disciplinary actions in accordance with the House Rules.

During our discussion, I noticed that I. V. was completely unfazed with the situation. She mentioned a few times that she "did nothing wrong". Because she "didn't use [her] powers on humans, [she] would never do that" (K. N. is a human student and has no knowledge of our world). How the "Satanic" symbols she and her "friend" (emphasis on the word mine) drew on the walls of the bathroom were actually ancient Illyrian runes, now "completely useless, you couldn't summon a bora with it, much less ghosts". I rectified that we don't say *ghosts* like humans do, but instead use the umbrella term *Returned, for all types of the dead who come back*, however, I don't think she cares for it, since it means nothing to her personally. Unless someone calls her an *elf* to her face, she's not bothered with nomenclature.

I. V. said it was all a harmless joke, how "stupid human girls" are all terribly fascinated by this apparition of "the woman in white", and that they can't stop talking about L. H.'s experience. I won't write down the correct words that I. V. used when describing the behavior of the human students because it's highly inappropriate language for a teen to use, especially in front of an adult, but that is I. V. for you, always trying to provoke.

In the end, for me, the only important thing was that I. V. didn't use her fae magic to charm K. N. into doing something against her will. And I. V. claims that she didn't do anything, she merely overheard the students from 118 talking about summoning a ghost, and since she was "withering from boredom", she decided to join in the fun. Our mountain fairy told K. N., who was staying in the Dorm for the weekend while the other roommates went back home, that she'd found some "magical spells" on the web. I. V. invented the whole story about murdered souls being trapped here, since she also knows about the Dorm's urban legend, and that the Illyrian runes are going to release them. "It was a funny game, until that c*** came and interrupted us," I. V. concluded. I verbally reprimanded her for the use of the C word.

I. V. promised me that she will stop with these "ghostly"

activities and that, in the future, she won't join in if she sees something similar happening, and that she'll immediately inform me if she hears about other girls doing something like this again. I. V. promised me all of this, just like she'd promised me, on multiple occasions, that she won't use her powers on humans, so I believed her as much as I would a mora wishing me only sweet dreams, and I expect that this won't be the last talk on this topic we'll have.

Addendum, Monday, December 10th, 2012:

I discreetly checked out I. V.'s claims to make sure she wasn't lying. I dislike using my powers on students, but I. V.'s participation was alarming enough for me to see the past through K. N.—specifically, the events that transpired on Saturday. I'm not going to write what I saw in detail, because that would be a serious breach of her privacy and my brain is not a video recorder for you to use. I'll only say that, by taking a glimpse into her past, I've confirmed that she was truly acting of her own free will.

It's my opinion that I. V., usually accustomed to attention, as it is in the nature of the fae when among humans, was jealous of this "woman in white" nonsense and wanted to get some of the spotlight back on her. I also checked the runes in question—my colleague A. showed them to me on her phone—and concluded that they were, indeed, harmless. Just in case, I checked with my wife, who has a better understanding of runes, and she confirmed my opinion.

A scan of the notes written by the night watchman M. Z. left in the Notebook during the night shift from Monday the 26th to Tuesday the 27th, November, 2012.

21:00 Made a round of the whole building to check if all the windows were firmly closed.

22:48 I found L. H. in room 118. I made her go back to her room.

23:05 Heard a scratching noise in the bathroom on the first floor, girls' wing. It came from the walls. I left the note for the janitor to check for mice in the morning. I also found the writing "come to us and devour us" carved on the wooden window sill.

From 00:25-00:51 Signal from the cameras was faint from the storm, and I kept losing the feed. I saw that one of the girls on the first floor was standing in the hallway, but the feed cut short and for the next few minutes the signal was completely lost.

01:23 Because of the feed that kept on disappearing constantly, and the rain that heavily limited visibility outside of the guard tower, I didn't notice right away that I had a student out in the rain. But after catching a glimpse of something moving on one of the backyard cameras, between losing the signal, I decided to go and check it out, just in case. After some time, I found the student L. H. in the garden at the back of the dorm, kneeling under the dead chestnut tree. She was digging with her hands in the muddy ground, soaking wet from the storm, in her pajamas, seemingly unaware of the storm or my presence. She was startled when I called her name, and told me she'd sleepwalked. I helped her go back to the Dorm.

A scan of my personal note in the special, unofficial notebook we keep on magical creatures enrolled in this Dorm and on other weird happenings around this place, Tuesday the 27th, 2012.

The previous night one of the human students apparently sleepwalked all the way to the chestnut tree that has the central place in the huge garden behind the Dorm. I confirmed the night watchman's written notes by checking the video footage myself, as much as I was able to, since the majority of the footage was useless, but I did follow the student in question going to the back garden.

This is concerning. Why that place in particular? The creepy tree is always filled with chestnuts that never fall, and my predecessors have underlined in this same notebook, multiple times, how important it is not to touch the shells growing on the branches but leave them be. I'm not happy with those instructions, mostly because it's getting increasingly more difficult to brush away the growing suspicions of the human faculty, who have learned to live with the fact that sometimes weird stuff happens on this ground. I would rather they be blissfully unaware. But also because I hate how the previous magical educators apparently just left the thing there. It emanates evil. I really should've checked it out by this point, but there was no time.

It's even more concerning when we take into account that the now overgrown and neglected garden had thrived the most when in the care of the cult, masquerading as nuns who used to practice human ritual sacrifice for their monstrous god residing in the Adriatic sea.

There's not much left about the cult thanks to WW2 destroying most of the evidence and our magical community not yet being shaped the way we are today. The majority of what we know are whispers, gossip, complaints lodged to the local krsnik protecting Rijeka at that time, and a bunch of missing persons cases leading straight to the walls of their nunnery. The few of the photos that managed to survive the bombing and looting are the only tangible evidence of their unholy activities. And thanks to some eyewitness testimony, we know that in the back of the nunnery the nuns grew various vegetables and fruits, all of which were destroyed by the Italian army when they drove the cult away. All of their hard work in the soil ended up rotting with time, and turned foul, leaving behind dead trees and weeds.

Out of all the places in the Dorm, the student went right there. I don't like that. I tried talking with L. H., but the girl was adamant that she was sleepwalking and in her past I could only see what she said herself—she exited her room, without a word, looking at something ahead of her and, stepping slowly, went right outside to the garden, ignoring the heavy rain that pelted her or the fact that she was stumbling in her slippers on the wet mud, came to stand before the chestnut tree, transfixed, for few seconds, then knelt and grabbed at the ground with her hands, her eyes firmly on the soil. She was doing that until the night watchman found her, covered in mud and soaking wet.

Up until he came, L. H. was alone, and not a word was muttered.

I also checked the original incident, something I'd believed I didn't have a need to do before. Again, I couldn't see the woman in white, but I could see L. H.'s reaction to something, definitely. She wasn't acting, or better said, I doubt she's that good of an actress. The pure dread in her face was unmistakable—the way her eyes opened so much I thought they were popping out of their sockets, how her body tightened as a rubber band stretching to the breaking point, before she let out a throat-shredding scream with the entirety of her lung capacity.

When talking with her educator, A., she admitted to me that she's concerned about L. H.'s wellbeing, but she wouldn't be the first student to have trouble with sleepwalking and that they'll find a way to keep it in check.

To do: go over the documentation I have on the Dorm's past, with a focus on the cult and garden. Learn more about L. H. At this point, there's not enough information for me to do more than that, but now I'm sure that there's something supernatural at play here, not just a prank or mere sleepwalking.

The report of the interview I had with my charge, the student I. V., written down after the fact, Thursday, November 29th, 2012.

My charge, I. V., showed up to my office early on Thursday to snitch on K. N. and L. H. The fae kept hanging out with K. N. and came to me claiming she had some "hot" new information. In return, I was to give her certain benefits. I agreed to her terms and conditions, mostly because I believed I should reward her good behavior, hoping to find a way we could connect, but also because I was concerned over L. H.'s incident and desperately needed a hint that would help me understand what is happening. (**Addendum, Monday, December 10th, 2012:** To better understand how stuck I was at the point, I had spent Tuesday and Wednesday going through moldy old papers and walking around the desolated back garden, circling the big chestnut tree with its black bark, whose branches were decorated with the thorny green shells even this far into November, as if the tree would start speaking to me, but learning nothing from its still presence. I decided that I need to cut the tree down—not only was it a sore sight, but also, I'm exhausted by how absolutely wrong it feels on my skin by just watching it. Before I could continue on with that idea, I. V. came to my office with just the thing I needed.)

I. V. shared with me how K. N. was constantly in contact with L. H., "she became L.'s shadow, honestly", supporting her ghost stories and promising any help L. H. needed to get in contact with "the woman in white". That was probably why L. H confided in K. N. that she didn't actually sleepwalked during the great storm on Monday night. The story I. V. got out was that L. H. woke up to "the woman in white" standing over her bed, and instead of waking her roommates, or screaming, L. H. got quietly out of bed and tried to touch the ghost. In turn, the ghost pivoted and started moving, "flickering", away, and L. H. followed her around the Dorm. It was the woman who brought her to the tree in the garden, but L. H. can't explain why she started digging, only that she felt the burning urge to do it. L. H. begged K. N. not to tell anyone, and K. N. begged I. V. not to share what was told to her in confidence, but I. V. recognized the opportunity to get something for herself, which brought her to me.

The other thing of interest was that L. H. wasn't scared anymore, but much more curious over the whole thing, wanting to learn more about "the woman in white" and why she'd brought her to the tree. She wants to find a way to communicate with the ghost, and K. N., of course, told her about I. V.'s magical runes for ghost summoning. So now the two came to the brilliant idea to hide tonight in the bathroom and, using the drawings of Illyrian symbols, try to get into contact with the ghost and ask her what she wanted from L. H.

K. N. asked I. V. to join them, but I. V. excused herself. "I did promise you not to do that," I. V. said to me, all sweet smiles which,

I would like to note, I do not trust. But she did a good thing by reporting this to me, which I wrote down in her student file so I can award her at the end of the school year (my unofficial file, of course).

Scan of my personal note in my special notebook, Thursday, November 29th, 2012.

I had an interview with I. V. over the new information brought to me about L. H.'s strange behavior.

Conclusion: if it's true that L. H. followed some kind of image of "the woman in white" only she can see, it could be a case of the incorporeal Returned. While there could be an argument made for the lack of the woman in the video footage during the storm, when the night watchman noted problems with the camera signal, it wouldn't explain the first incident when the cameras worked fine. And if there was someone with her both times, they would show up in my visions of the past.

This brings me to the conclusion of incorporeal Returned—they are only a phantom imprint sometimes visible to the sensitive eye, so it would make sense why I couldn't see it in the river of time or the video footage. But that would mean L. H. had some inkling of magic in her that I've missed, and that could be a problem. Humans generally aren't sensitive enough to catch a glimpse at the incorporeal Returned, much less follow them around.

To do: learn more about L. H., find a way to confirm if it's really a Returned and if L. H. has magic, and then decide what to do with the information.

The report of the interview I had with L. H., written down after the fact, Thursday, November 29th, 2012.

I found L. H. in the library, where I conducted my interview with her which I'm writing down. She was doing what I'd hoped she wouldn't be—searching for the book on the history of the Dorm.

When I asked what she was searching for, and said I could maybe help her, she shrugged and tried to act nonchalant, saying she was interested in history and that our Dorm had "an intriguing past" but that there's not a lot of information about it online, and maybe there would be in some book. I could see that she was nervous, her arms slightly shaking; she was avoiding eye contact with me, hiding her face behind her long hair. At this point, I was focusing very hard on what my eyes weren't seeing, hunting for that hint of magic. For that sense of a centipede crawling under the skin, burrowing in the tender meat, of the chilly needless puncturing lungs and leaking the air out through the membranes, of the roots of the teeth coming loose, breaking off from the gums in gushes of blood.

I didn't feel anything so drastic, except for the slightest discomfort, the skin of my palms itching, irritably. It was easy to miss it, dismiss it as a normal bodily function, like when my skin reacted to scratchy clothes. I note this here as descriptively as I can, so if anyone were to read this report, they would understand why it was so easy for me to fail to notice that L. H. had magic, previous to this encounter. It was so imperceptible that she couldn't do much with it, I would bet. As far as I or the Council knew, when she enrolled in the Dorm, there were no recorded magical beings in the village she comes from, so there was no need for me to work with her. I assume that the line of magic she belongs to had probably lost contact with our community generations before, which is why she doesn't know about us, or we about her.

I asked her whether she was searching for something specific. She didn't want to talk with me, I could see that, which is not surprising. I've never worked directly with her before, and she only knew me as an educator who sometimes comes to the girls' wing to talk with her colleagues. To give her a reason to confide with me, I told her that I could maybe help her because my grandparents were very enthusiastic about Rijeka's history and know a lot of things that aren't in books. How my granny was a teen when the Dorm was abandoned after World War II—for that brief period of time it had served as barracks for the Italian army—and how she remembered coming here to the bombing wreckage.

That got L. H. talking. She admitted that she was interested in an even farther past, before the Italian army, at the beginning of the 20th century when the Dorm was a nunnery. She told me that she had hoped to find photos from that period, what the Dorm looked like, the church that had stood here before bombs destroyed it, if there was a photo of the nuns, things like that.

I would like to note here that all of these were the things I didn't want the students to be digging into.

I told her that I didn't know if any photos from that period survived, and that there's certainly no books or documentation from that period in the Dorm's library, since the Italian army had ransacked the nunnery when they took over the place, and then the City cleaned out everything else that had stayed behind them before turning the building into a dormitory for highschoolers. I asked her whether this fascination has anything to do with the story the older students are telling, about the killer nuns. That was the wrong thing to say because L. H. closed down, growing even shyer than before, turning away from me. I tried to explain that I wasn't judging, how I understand the curiosity, but she wasn't in the mood to talk with me anymore and excused herself from the conversation.

Addendum, Monday, December 10th, 2012: If you wish to ask me why I haven't used this opportunity to dig even deeper into L. H.'s past, I would like to point out that, without knowing what I'm searching for, I could get lost in time, sifting through countless memories, my body standing there in the library as a statue; or even worse, it would induce a seizure, which is something I want to avoid.

The report of the interview I had with A. B., written down after the fact, Thursday, November 29th, 2012.

I told my colleague A. B. that a student had come forward to me about L. H. and K. N.'s plan of nightly ghost summonings in the bathroom. My assessment was that it would be the best course of action to share that bit of information with A. I used that as an opening to poke around L. H. and her family, since I knew there must be a connection between the magical community and the student's family that I kept missing. Simple questions, what her parents were doing, if A. knew what kind of people they were—prone to superstition, religion, something in that line that could influence the girl to believe in ghosts.

Most of the information that my colleague relayed was mundane and there's no reason to waste time writing it down. But what piqued my interest, and what I will report here, is that there was a connection between her family and Rijeka that I didn't know before.

L. H. wasn't the first generation to be in our Dorm. Her mother had also been enrolled here during high school education and that was the reason L. H. came to us instead of choosing a dormitory much closer to the medical school (such as Podmurvice Dormitory or Kvarner Dormitory—both are within walking distance from the medical school, unlike our Dorm, which is situated much farther, on the outskirts of the city, where she has to rely on the bus line to get to and back from the school). A. tiredly noted that in her last conversation with the mother—a phone call after the sleepwalking during the storm—she also learned an interesting tidbit of family lore and connection to the Dorm. How L. H.'s great-grandma joined the nunnery, and about some "sort of scandal" regarding teen pregnancy. "Her great-grandma died a young nun, tuberculosis."

I'm trying to recreate word for word what A. said. It seems that, while the great-grandmother was sick, she wrote to her family begging them to take her baby if "something were to happen to her." She probably knew she wouldn't pull through, and L.'s mother assumes she didn't want the child adopted by some wealthy Italian family."

L. H.'s mom said it was the reason she came to this Dorm in the first place, to "keep up with the tradition", "feel closer to her family's past", which A. admits seems "morbid" given that the nun tragically died in the same place. But A. also notes that L. H.'s mother has now, after all this woman in white "nonsense", changed her mind and doesn't find it a "cool tradition", but more of a burden, and she wants for L. H. to change the dorms. The mother believes that it was the mix of bleak family stories with the student urban legend that created vivid nightmares for her daughter. Regardless, L. H. isn't keen to move.

I asked my colleague if she was absolutely certain that L. H.'s great-grandmother was a nun in this particular nunnery and not with the Benedictines who also had a base in Rijeka, and A. confirmed that yes, that was what L. H.'s mother said to her.

After this, A. went in search of K. N. and L. H. to have a long talk about their night plans, and I went to check the photos of the nunnery my grandmother still has.

The report of the interview I had with L. H., written down after the fact, Friday, November 30th, 2012.

I conducted this interview with the student L. H. inside the library. We were alone at the time of our conversation. L. H was surprised that I had to talk with her, and it was obvious she was uncomfortable. I know that my colleague, A., had managed to foil L. H. and K. N.'s plans for the previous night, and that they had a cleaning assignment in the bathrooms as a punishment.

Now, if there comes a time in the future when this report ends up in the hands of the Council, I'm going to assume that this is the part they might not like. But it was an important thing to do, and I stand by it.

I gave the girl an old photo showing the nuns from the cult. The gray color of the photo has been slowly eaten away by the years, fading, depicting a group of fifty or so nuns, still identifiable. Or, if we're going to be technical, a group of people dressed in habit-like dresses that could pass for any Catholic order. They all stood before a church that looked like any other church—nothing more, nothing less—in four rows, arranged by height.

I told L. that the photo came from my grandmother, which was correct, and that I can't give it to her, but that I would very much like to hear the story of her great-grandmother. L. was, well, I wouldn't say happy, but showed a nervous energy and excitement for the photo. She watched it closely for a few minutes. I was contemplating searching through her past in the meantime, but gave up on the idea, unsure of the correct time and date I should be focusing on.

L. finally said that she found her great-grandmother and pointed to one woman surrounded by others. I'll note here that the woman in question was young, but a bit older than our students, with a tired look on her face as if she hadn't seen sleep in years. This is probably what you look like after a long night of slaughter, or when you expect that one day the sea monster you pray to will wake up and drown everyone in the city.

She didn't look pregnant in the photo and I wondered when it was taken.

I asked L. how she knew what her great-grandmother looked like. Did they have her photos at home? It wouldn't be impossible, but seemed quite unlikely. At this point, I already had an idea what might be happening, but waited for L. to confirm it.

At first, L. was reluctant to say anything to me, only shrugged and played with the photo in her hands. So I asked point blank if she recognized her because that was her woman in white. L. seemed startled with my questions, surprised and anxious, so I quickly assured her that I'm not like the others, that I believe her and that I wish to hear from her what is happening, and not the reinterpretations from her parents, or my colleagues, or other students. That there was no judgment on my part. She probably thought I was ridiculing her, but I managed to be convincing, sharing with her that my grandparents are highly spiritual people, and that they'd instilled in me the belief in the world outside of our own, and that I've also had some brushes with the things that can't be explained.

It was half-truths and half-lies, it's not like I straight up told her about the hidden magical community in Rijeka, or that a mountain fairy sleeps in a bed only a few rooms over from her. It was my gamble to tell even this much, and it was worth it. Better than to make the girl believe she was going through some sort of mental health crisis.

With a few carefully chosen words, I managed to get L. to see me as an ally, the only one who didn't dismiss her experience. Probably the only adult who told her that they believed that she saw the woman in white, and was truly *believing* in her account, no matter how impossible, and not in the way other students said they did, roleplaying belief because it was a shiny new game to play.

My strategy paid off because L. confided in me. What she had to say only strengthened my theories. Here are the important parts, following the timeline, which is not how our discussion went because I had to interrupt her with new questions, and she was constantly getting lost in digressions, but for easier reading, I will write it down chronologically.

1. The story goes that the nun had sent the letter to her own mother, admitting she'd had a baby, and how she's going to lose her if the nun's own family doesn't take her in. How she was sick and scared and wanted her child safe in her home. How she regretted ever joining the nunnery, how she had been a true believer, but now wasn't sure of anything anymore. All of that had been a great shock to the family, because after a few months of no contact, the content of this letter came with a bang, from the unexpected baby to the loss of faith, and no one in the family knew what to make of it. Never before did they have an inkling that something was wrong, or that there could be a secret pregnancy. Suffice to say, the family wasn't happy, father and the grandparents especially,

and didn't want to meddle, or take in a bastard baby that would shame them. The nun's mother (L.'s great-great-grandmother) went against the wishes of the rest, took what little money she could, and traveled completely alone to the big city, begging to see her daughter and grandchild.

By the time she came to the town, L.'s great-grandmother was already dead, and the nuns didn't let the mother to see her daughter's corpse, or to even know where her grave was. Apparently, L.'s great-grandmother had died from tuberculosis, but L. admitted that her grandmother didn't believe that, nor had her great-great-grandmother, who passed her suspicion down the family line.

The nuns didn't want to give up the baby, saying they'd already had plans for her, but L.'s great-great-grandma made a fuss, the loud kind, and the nuns relented. I'm going to assume they were attracting too much attention from the neighbors and local authorities, the kind they didn't want or need with their activities, and they decided it was better to drop the child and let them both leave. I wonder why they didn't simply kill L.'s great-great-grandmother and remove the nuisance that way. Maybe they were worried that it would only bring the next family member to their gates.

People were gossiping over the possible father of the child, but L. said that all of it was unconfirmed. L.'s great-grandmother hadn't mentioned him, and in fact, nobody knew she was pregnant until the letter came. The nuns didn't want to give up his identity, saying how it wasn't important anymore, since he was long gone and would reconnect with his child only in her death.

2. Jumping to the now, when L. came to the Dorm, the nightmares started. She claims that, before, she remembers having a true nightmare only a couple of times, but when she slept in the Dorm, they would come with frequency and vividness, unlike anything at home, or anywhere else. She would wake up gasping for air after particularly nasty dreams of drowning in the vast blue of the sea, still tasting salt. The drowning was an occurring nightmare and it was always the same—she would find herself in the dreams,

being dragged across a rocky beach by the the tight grip of invisible hands toward the turbulent waves, crashing down on her legs, hands forcing her head down, down, down, under the water, holding her while the sea assaulted her mouth, her nose and eyes, getting down her throat, collecting in her lungs, burning with salt.

She would always wake up when the burning in her chest grew too hot and unbearable, only to find her pillow thoroughly soaked with her tears.

Other times it was a different nightmare. She would find herself in the Dorm, her bare feet on the cold floor, following the echoing footsteps around her, trying to find someone, but not knowing whom. But the incessant thought that someone was calling her, waiting for her, was an irritating phantom itch, and she would spend the dream walking all over the Dorm, searching. Something was wrong with the Dorm, though, it wasn't exactly like in the waking world. The tiled floor was the same, decorated with blue shells. But the hallways were too long, too high, too twisted, going constantly in circles, and outside the windows, the only thing she could see were some kind of thin, sharp red branches of gnarled trees, but in her dream she knew that they weren't really trees. This second dream wasn't as bad as the first, and she would mostly just wake up tired, and with the relief that she didn't need to walk anymore.

3. When she first heard the story about the nuns killing people and stuffing them in the walls, she was insulted. She didn't want to explain to her roommates why, and kept to herself that her great-grandmother was one of the nuns because she didn't want her ancestor to become a joke.

L. admitted how, no matter her feelings on the matter, she did think there could be some truth to the urban legend. It just made sense to her, given the suspicious proceedings over the death of her great-grandmother. It was so easy to believe the evil nuns had killed her and stuffed her in the walls. The only thing missing was motive, and investigating the nunnery didn't yield any results.

Every single keyword she would google would bring her to the Benedictines, but they'd never been stationed in this Dorm and no matter how hard she tried searching the internet, she couldn't find any other order of nuns in Rijeka. She thought it would be easier if she knew their name, but neither L.'s mother or grandmother knew it—that tidbit of family lore had unexplainably been lost.

4. The night of the incident with the woman in white, L. wasn't afraid. Not right away. In those first few seconds, a sense of familiarity had hidden away any possible strangeness of the encounter. The thought that came to her was "finally", like she'd found something lost a long time ago, something she had search for all over the Dorm, under the beds, in the accumulating dust, in the grime of the bathroom floor, in the plates of her meals, the shrubbery of the garden, and deep inside the walls.

It was only when her brain started noticing the little things—the flickering, the unnatural stillness of the woman's face, the soundlessness of her words, the water pouring out of her mouth, the floating over the floor, that L.'s flight of fight instinct kicked in, and she had fled, overflowing with the worst fear she had ever felt in her life.

5. L. knew she wasn't sleeping or sleepwalking, but started to lie simply to get everyone off her back. Especially when it seemed that the principal believed the night watchman that L. had taken some drugs. The "nightmare" story was much easier, more agreeable to all the adults.

Even though she was afraid of the woman in white and what seeing her meant, L. wanted to come back to the Dorm, even though her parents weren't sure after the whole mess with the principal. She was now firm in her decision to find out as much as she could about the history of the nunnery and what happened to her ancestor. With meager information available, she decided to go right to the source—the woman in white, who she'd started to suspect was her great-grandmother—while she was recuperating at home. It seems the woman in white had similar ideas, because the first night L. was back in the dorm, the ghost came to her for the second time.

L. couldn't fall asleep with the storm trashing outside the windows, her brain convinced it was the Adriatic itself, arising from the coast to crash its waves on the walls of the Dorm, bashing until stone crumbles to dust, to drag all the sleeping students from their beds to the depths of the sea to join... something. L. wasn't sure what.

While turning in her bed, head swimming in disturbing images, she sensed the presence in the room with her, not her roommates, but someone else, standing there, by her bed. By the light of her phone, she could see it was the woman in white. Her great-grandmother stood still—and L. now unmistakably knew it was her, knowing that with her whole being. The woman looked similar to how she'd first appeared, except her hair was drenched. So was her face, little streams flowing down her mouth and eyes like a fountain, forming in a puddle under L.'s bed.

L., not as afraid now as she was the first time, got out of bed. She wanted to touch her great-grandmother's ghost, try and speak with her. But the woman flickered in and out, getting out of her reach.

Similar to her second dream, where she was following someone, so was L. now following the woman in white through the dorm, the lightning from the storm hiding her own echoing steps. For a moment, L. was worried this was just another wandering nightmare, but the ghost continued to walk out of the Dorm, and L.'s dreams never went that far from the hallways.

Through the freezing storm and almost complete darkness, she followed the woman in white, who glowed with blurry, dim white light, to the big ugly garden behind the Dorm, overgrown with bushes and thorns that kept catching on L.'s pajamas and scratching her legs. They walked until the ghost suddenly stopped before a ghoulish tree at the center of the garden. To L.'s eyes, the tree pulsed with darkness, and she could hear its thrumming through the rain and thunderstorm. Her stomach was roiling with her steps getting her closer to the tree and the ghost who kept her back turned to L.

Through the dark, L. could see the glowing hand of the woman in white rising toward the bark of the tree. When her fingers came into contact with it, the ghost burst as a bubble, transforming into a gush of water splashing the ground and L., and she could taste salt on her lips and knew it wasn't just any water, but the sea from her dreams.Whatever light there was suddenly disappeared and L. became acutely aware she was standing in the downpour of a freezing storm, goosebumps prickling her skin, from the top of her head to the bottom of her soles.

Yet her body couldn't move, or at least, not in the direction she would want to go, back to the safety of her room. Instead, the strong urge to dig in the ground at her feet overcame her senses, as if her body knew something she didn't, her legs and arms moving of their own accord, dropping her on her knees in front of the tree, her fingers grabbing at the mud, opening up a hole. She couldn't break from her mission, whatever it was, until the night watchman called her name, and only that had snapped her out of it, and her body came back under her control.

6. And this brought L. to the idea of summoning the woman in white with K. N. She was now sure her great-grandmother wanted to communicate something to her. L. didn't know how to do it, though, but her friend, K. N., was also interested in contacting the spirit world, and even claimed that the other student, I.V., found some obscure rituals that L. couldn't find anywhere on the web, to do it. Except, their educator, A. B., somehow found out about their plans, and chewed their heads off.

After the threat of expulsion from the Dorm, L. and K. N. agreed to abandon their plan. Regardless, L. wants to find a way to communicate with the ghost of her great-grandmother. She believes the woman was murdered and her ghost is calling for justice, and to help her move on to the afterlife, L. needs to find out what had happened to her.

The woman in white hasn't come back, but L. believes it's only a matter of time before she appears again, and next time,

L. would be much better prepared.

This brings us to the conversation with me in the library. Now, L. believes she's found an ally in an adult, and her relief was obvious. L. seems headstrong and capable, the little I could see from her, so I fully believe she will find a way to dig the truth out with a little help from her Returned great-grandmother. This is unacceptable and further actions need to be taken.

A scan of my personal note in my special notebook, Friday, November 30th, 2012.

Course of action: banishing the Returned.

I asked both my krsnik contact and my štriga wife for advice. I had hoped that a simple blessing of the grounds could do the trick, but both of them agreed—a shock that a krsnik and a štriga agreed on something instead of fighting to the death, which really shows the validity of the information—that it doesn't work on the Returned. Incorporeal Returned come back for three main reasons: unfinished business, great injustice, or guilt. Figure out the reason, take care of it, and the Returned will move on. In this case, my conclusion is this:

Given the nature of the letter L.'s great-grandmother had sent to her family, it's my fair assumption that her Return is the result of either injustice or guilt, or maybe a combination of both. Taking into consideration the recurring motifs of water and drowning in L.'s story, I think it's safe to assume they had drowned her, either because she'd lost her faith, or because they'd disagreed over the baby, or something else. Maybe she felt guilt over her part in ritualistic killings and that's the driving factor behind her Return.

The fact that she's found a way to connect to her descendant was not lost on me. I believe that, whatever magic the nuns possessed, it managed to get passed down to L. too. Not counting the amulets and other similarly infused tools, we know that magic is either hereditary, or born to. The magic of the sea creature or the old god, or whatever it was the nuns prayed to, sacrificed for power, could've manifested in L.

stronger than in her mother, helping her see her Returned ancestor.

In any case, if I can't give the woman in white what she needs and she sticks to the grounds, I asked if there was a way to protect L. H. from her Returned ancestor. My wife believes there's a type of curse that I could invoke, and my krsnik contact says that there's a type of blessing I can bestow, but both of them agree that, to do that, I need to use something that had been a part of the woman in white—preferably from her body, like bone, tissue, blood, hair, rather than a possession which can be faulty if it hadn't been of importance to her life.

What that means in practice is that I need to make a talisman from the remains. It won't banish her to the afterlife, but it will cut her connection to L. H. and leave the girl in peace. The nuns didn't record the location of the grave. In fact, we don't even know where they buried their dead or their victims. Their whole shtick was the Adriatic sea and placating their monster at the bottom of it, so we always assumed they simply dumped their dead to the sea.

If L.'s great-grandmother's remains are at the bottom of the Adriatic feeding the fish, I'll need to find a new way. But I have a suspicion regarding the grave, at least if the Return of the dead nun is connected to her untimely death. Of course, there's a chance L. was compelled to dig under the chestnut tree for some other reason, but I'll soon learn if it was a correct or incorrect assumption.

Incident report regarding the case of the Returned and my findings under the chestnut tree that occurred on Saturday, December 1st, written on Monday, December 3rd, 2012, on the behest of the Council.

Before taking any action, I talked with the principal and gave him basic information on the events, to keep him in the loop and out of my way. Of course, the information I gave him was heavily redacted, but enough to give me space to do whatever I have to do.

The principal closed down the dorm for the weekend under the excuse of repairs of the heavy water damage after the recent storm that hit Rijeka. That left me alone with the Dorm and all of its dead.

When I came to the grounds, it was immediately obvious to me that the place was bristling with malicious energy, leaving a touch of unpleasant ache on my nape. The Dorm's yellow facade painfully burned in the gloom of the heavy, dark clouds hanging over the towering roof. For a moment, I could even catch a glimpse of the church, once connected to the Dorm, superimposed over the parking lot that now stood in its place, and while focusing on it, the colorful stained glass windows slowly solidified before my eyes, with a hint of shifting humanoid shadows moving behind it. After a second or two, the vision disappeared, the church's bell tower wavering like smoke, before it all blended in the background of the Dorm, erased from my sight.

In the garden, the air around me drank up my steps, rendering my movements soundless. Above my head, the clouds weren't just dark gray, they were almost pitch black, rendering the colors mute and dead. The overgrown grass was wet, and stank heavily of iron and salt. In the center, a huge chestnut tree stood with its mangled limbs littered with new thorny shells. Usually, I keep clear of it, not touching the thing, as it was advised to me, but now I wanted to see what would actually happen if I tried to pick a never-falling shell, what secrets they hide inside their husks.

When I grabbed at one, I saw that the chestnut shell was fused to the branch and didn't bulge. I had to pull all my strength trying to dislodge it—yes, yes, I know, it wasn't very smart of me to do that—and for my efforts, I only ended up shredding the skin of my left palm, which shouldn't have been possible, because the burrs are sharp, but they aren't steel-sharp. And yet. It's a good thing the air absorbed my shrieks and curses, because otherwise, I think I would've been heard all the way down our hill to the sea.

While I was standing there, clutching my bleeding arm like the idiot that I am, the shell I'd tried to break apart from the tree opened with a wet *pop*, and a purple appendage squirmed out from the crack, rotten teeth growing along its length. It licked away my blood and skin tissue left on the burrs from my efforts. When the last drop was collected, the swollen cancerous tongue wriggled back inside the shell, the surface of it closing down like a clam. This was new information for me, but then again, never did I try to touch the tree, much less try to open the shells with my blood. At that moment, I knew I'd made a great mistake by ignoring the tree like my predecessors had.

I decided that the first order of action was that the tree must go down, because there was no way I would dig under the tree filled with teeth hungry for my blood, not knowing what to expect from the evil thing once I start messing close to its roots. Since the Dorm was empty and I had no one to help me, I took an electric saw from our custodian's shack.

I needed exactly an hour to take the damn tree down, leaving only a stump. It didn't help that my left hand was mangled, or that it felt as if the bark was constantly fighting back against the electric teeth of the saw while it whirled and whirled and ate deeper into the wood. I won't bore you with unnecessary details of my whole ordeal that kept me in the garden for the entirety of the day. After the sawing of the tree, the ground was covered in fallen shells and my boots were leaving purple smears and a crackling sound of shattered teeth. The digging left me bruised, aching, and covered in dirt that I could even taste and breathe in. But, as you've heard from my initial verbal report, when all was done, I found not only the resting place of L.'s great-grandmother, as I'd expected, but much, much more.

The first bone—a human skull with a few missing molars and a sinewy root piercing it through the eye socket—was relatively close to the surface and I almost destroyed it with the shovel. After that, I was more careful.

I'll say it right away—I have no idea how deep the grave goes. I only managed to dig out the surface level, and the more that I uncovered, the more roots I found with their ghoulish decorations, and the worse it went. One skull was suddenly four, one of which was small and packed with two additional rows of teeth in the jaw, long bones of arms and legs, two fragmented rib cages, and numerous flat, short bones that I couldn't identify since I'm not a medical professional. But what was worrying is that all of the bones I found were impaled on the roots, making it a disturbing decoration for the tree, almost like beads on a beard. Trying to dislodge bone matter from the roots only caused the roots to pulse and wiggle under my palms, wet and fat, shifting bones from the surface into its own mess of roots and earth. I could feel the ground under me quivering, opening up like jaws, giving me a glimpse of the living, coiling roots interconnected with the bones like a nest of snakes, and I sensed its hunger as if it were my own.

I thought that, after killing L.'s great-grandmother, they buried her in the garden because she used to be one of them. But she wasn't alone in her grave. We were wrong about the nuns dumping victims into the sea, and by accident, I found them. My educated guess is that the roots feed on the cult's victims buried in the ground. The cursed chestnut tree grew under the ground, snatching up whatever it could find, even now, half a century later, when the only thing left from the sacrifices were bones. It didn't care that the nunnery had changed hands. It didn't care that I'd killed its body when I took down the trunk. It refused to die.

I don't know what kind of an action we should take to get it out completely. It would probably require digging out a huge chunk of the garden, and I'm honestly worried what we could find if we do this. A whole sea of bodies is my guess. And I'm not exaggerating. While I was immersed in my findings, concentrating on keeping the writhing roots at a safe distance from my skin, I'd attracted an unexpected audience, which I only noticed when I finally crawled out of the hole I'd dug out.

They stood in a semicircle surrounding the tree, completely still. Wearing now vintage clothing, old skirts and trousers, mostly rugged and worn-out cloth, faces blank, eyes boring right into me. In thin hands, some wrinkled with time, some smooth and young, they held candles the dim flames of which were soundlessly flickering in the shadow of the dark, hanging clouds. Children—ranging from small ones whose ages I have no idea how to discern to preteens—peeked behind the adults, with the same blank masks, devoid of emotions. I know, rationally, that the Returned don't actually have any emotions. The ability to feel something ended when their nerves and organs shut down forever. Irrationally, I read their blank faces as those of judgment.

Never in my life had I seen so many Returned in one place. I knew of stories of the processions of the dead but I'd never experienced one. This gathering was so large I couldn't count them. This is how I know what is under the garden. If we were to try and dig everyone out, we would have to close the Dorm down for a few days, maybe even weeks, and, at worst, months, since the chestnut tree is proving to have strong magic, thanks to all the death it's sucked on during long periods of time. It wouldn't let us get it away from the bones easily, or out of the ground. And we could risk the information leaking. This wouldn't be easy to contain, would require the work of multiple people, and you know very well how it goes in our community. And it would be even worse if the wrong person learned of our efforts and the humans in Rijeka discovered what was right under this hill. Better not risk it, and leave this mass grave covered up.

This isn't ideal, of course, I know that. I knew it watching the collection of faces before me, trust me. Young and old, they all came to me in a quiet gathering, and even without a spoken word, without any emotion possibly cursing through their phantom bodies, I knew that their wish for a closure was keeping them locked in the place where they'd met their violent ends. To fix their great injustice would be to tell their stories, to get their bodies out and give them a proper burial, far from the place they were slaughtered. But I've already told you my opinion on the matter, and I already knew at that moment, no matter how heavy my heart was, that it would be an impossible task, at least right now.

I hope there will come a day when we can give them the closure they seek.

I told them I'm sorry, even though it is meaningless and it helps no one.

But let's get back to the important part. Because I know what you're wondering, and yes, she was there too. In the sea of colorful garments clustering around her, the simple white dress was easy to spot. Her face was the same blank paper as the others' and it was so hard to recognize the young woman from the photo in this faint impression reflecting back only nothingness. Small seashells, seagrass, and red corals with long, pointy polyps were tangled in her long hair cascading free down her shoulders and back. She was the only one dressed like this, as much as I could see, but it was hard to discern details in the darkening day and with such a big mass of apparitions.

The new storm was fast approaching so I knew I had to speed up my efforts, just like I need to finish writing this report before it turns into an epistolary novel. I just want to be sure that all of the details are jotted down, all i's dotted and so on.

The Returned parted for me with the simplicity of long grass bending out of the way. The sensation their closeness left on my person was one of harsh winter cold whispering in my ears. I got right to our woman in white, whose expression didn't change, didn't falter. Others closed in around us, all turned toward me, as if watching closely what I'm doing. Even though I knew they couldn't do anything to me, I'll admit to you, I was a bit worried, an irrational claustrophobia locking down my lungs. For a moment or two, it was difficult to breathe, as if I'd found myself submerged under water, and for a brief second, my sight did slip to the past, to the blurry gloom and the panicked trashing inside the ceremonial well, a group of stern-faced nuns standing above it, one crying baby in their arms, while the woman in white drowned, drowned, drowned. The vision slipped past, and the woman before me opened her mouth to a wriggling coral growing from inside, out of her, and weaving like a snake sniffing the air. Tears or water droplets leaked from her eyes down her cheeks. In the smell of upcoming rain, I could hear a murmur, an echo from the past—*if she'd been a true believer, she wouldn't have drowned. It was all we needed to know. Instead, the water got inside, clogged up her lungs, then spat her body back out to us.*

I assume it was another glimpse, auditory instead of the visual ones that I usually get, and that I'd heard the rationale that nuns gave to each other, or maybe someone else.

In the present, I asked the woman in white if she could help me find her remains. Of course, it was a foolish hope on my part. It's not like the phantom before me could dig a hole to her bones. She just stood there while corals grew from her throat, breaking out from the mouth, rising in the air, slowly but steadily, thin red lines like crystallized blood. Her head twisted upward, eyes now fixed on the sky above, her body and hair dripping with more and more water, as if she was getting soaked from invisible rain. Sea shells bloomed in her lush hair, white and cream, and even small crabs crawled out from the straight locks on her forehead, walking over her eyes.

When the cold drizzle started hitting my cheeks—nowhere near the biting chill emanating from the Returned around me—I got scared I wouldn't be able to do anything of consequence to help her move on. I couldn't give her closure, I couldn't do that to any of the specters around me. Not on my own, and not in such a short time. But, maybe I could help bring her peace, ensuring that she can keep close to her family, reunited in a way, protecting them always, not as a Returned, but like more of a blessing. Or a curse.

I admit, I'd consulted with my krsnik contact over the phone, right there, standing on the open wound of the mass grave with the writhing roots behind my back—churning mud between its tendrils—while rain started to pour mercilessly, falling through the flickering images of the Returned, their phantom candles with live phantom flames, unconcerned with the rain. You can check with the krsnik, I can leave you their phone number.

Anyway, after that short consultation, I had to do perhaps the hardest part. With freezing arms, one of which was already wounded and slick with spilled blood, I got back to the hole I'd dug out. At least it was easy to slide back in, the living roots pulling the ground toward its depths, me with it. I'm not going to bore you with all the details but, careful not to get tangled in its grasp, I managed to carve out a piece of one wriggling dark root with a knife. I couldn't get to the bones, but my guess was, and still is, that all of the root system was connected to them, all of the remains. As I mentioned before, it's my assumption that the tree is feeding on the corpses of the deceased, getting strong magic from their deaths. So I assumed that, even if I couldn't find the bones from the woman in white, I didn't actually need them if I had a piece of the root fat on the juices from her body and death. Maybe even a piece of bark would do, but it wasn't as alive as the roots that were actively trying to tie me up in their ropes, so I didn't want to risk having to dig again. Once I put the ground back over the roots, I promised to myself not to disturb it anymore.

With the severed piece of the root that was weeping ink-dark mucus all over me, I closed the mass grave. The Returned came closer to me, bringing a wave of freezing air that was sucking out my breaths. They stood still, like stone sculptures in the Adriatic, covered in algae and seagrass, their eyes the black holes of deep ocean, or maybe the stomach of a monster, sleeping on the seabed to the lullaby of the busy town and angry seagulls. The sharp red corals growing out from the woman in white's mouth were forming a canopy over her head, blooming with sea anemones instead of flowers. Her body was breaking out in mussels, urchins, and crawling crabs. I knew I had to ignore the image, otherwise I would have stood there a witness to her transformation for the remainder of the day, and maybe the night, and who knows how it would have ended. So I cut it short when I pushed in the last grain of the ground I'd uncovered from the roots, burying it all again—the roots, the bones, the Returned.

They all disappeared with that, including her.

Dirty, muddy, and bloody, it was late afternoon that I got out of the garden, the felled trunk of the chestnut tree with its treetop left on the ground, only a stump still firmly fixed and defiant, and the overturned earth the hint of what has been done.

I went, straight away, to my krsnik contact, who carved the piece of the root, pulsing hot and slick even hours after getting cut from the rest, into something resembling a thin pendant, curling like a spiral, and engraved into it a miniscule script in the old Slavic language, as dead as the woman in white. I can't write down the exact words, but it was a prayer for L. to be safe from all the specters of the past, shielding her from wandering Returned and the sins of her ancestors, giving her only peaceful dreams, through the blood and bones of her great-grandmother, ingested in the root as they were. My contact assured me this would also mean that the woman in white shouldn't appear to L. anymore. The woman wouldn't be able to move on, forever bound now to the piece of root, now a sacred talisman. They said that L. should keep it on herself at all times.

It's my proposal, and my contact agrees with me, to use the trunk I left in the garden to carve out a sculpture I can infuse with my magic to work as a protection ward on the entirety of the Dorm's territory. With my efforts, it could cast a large net over the Dorm, potent from all the death magic it ate through the roots. I will destroy the rest, but it would be a shame to burn it all since it could be quite a powerful tool.

This is why I'd contacted you initially, asking for help. I can carve the necessary faces and say all the important prayers, but this spell asks for more than even I can give, and with your help, we can close the circle and use something evil to do something good, and shelter these kids who live here from all who would want them harm.

I gave L. H. the talisman today, early in the morning, and some falsified letters I'd written on Sunday. I spun some tale how my grandmother, after hearing about L. and her great-grandma, found them in the city's archive. The necklace, I said to L., was from her great-grandma, and it was important for her to wear, to keep her ghost close and calm, knowing that her bloodline lives on. The falsified letters told a story of her dying great-grandma, writing about her terrible lung sickness, and how she knew that she wouldn't manage to survive, hoping her family would take her baby, rather than for her daughter to be adopted by strangers. Why those letters never came to L. H.'s family, who could know, I explained to L. A lot of things could have happened, including the nuns punishing her great-grandmother for the disgrace of pregnancy. I fed that and much more to the girl, until I was certain she accepted it all and believed me with the gullibility of a teen.

In the end, after shedding a few tears over my masterpiece of forgery, she promised me that she will wear the necklace to honor her great-grandmother, which is all I needed. We'll see if this will finally be the end of the woman in white.

Addendum, Friday, December 7th, 2012:

A week passed without incident. Well, real incidents. L. H. didn't see her great-grandma, nor did she have new nightmares, but there were still the "woman in white" summoning games played by other students. A.'s written reprimands morphed into creative punishments, like garden work (not in the backyard, but at the front), cleaning of the Dorm, and making ceramics bowls, and it won't stop until the games stop, and the principal is completely done with this all, and is on the verge of calling actors to playact exorcism. K. N. calmed down, getting bored with no results from her summonings, except worse and worse punishments.

Unfortunately, the story of the woman gained a new version among my magical students, courtesy of I. V. The mountain fae, in a last bid for importance, if I had to guess, started a rumor that the "woman in white" is a Returned of a sacrificed victim, and how she roams the halls at night, searching for students out of bed to eat them alive.

Since it's not even close to the truth and is only an upgrade of an existing urban legend, I'm going to let it slide.

Addendum, Monday, December 10th, 2012: The clawing sounds turned out to be a rat infestation and that is being taken care of.

Addendum, Monday, December, 10th 2012: These are all of my reports and notes regarding the "woman in white" incident. For further information, check with my krsnik contact who can explain in more detail what we want to do with the protection ward. I hope this clears any misinformation you had about the involvement of magical students, and how I work. I know I'm not the most conventional protector this place has had.

I hope to hear soon from you, whether you'll let me go, or help me with the chestnut sculpture.

Phone call overheard by the rats in the walls and the lonely Returned in their restless afterlife:

Nana:

"Hey, honey, sorry, didn't see your messages, yeah, yeah, I'm just writing the stupid reports and interviews...

...No, I was supposed to have it all written after the fact, but who the fuck cares about it. Nobody usually asks me for anything... so I just kind of left it all piled up? And now I need to fake *all* of the stupid documentation for the fuckers.

... No, of course not, no way I'm going to tell them that you and the girl were with me that night in the garden. I'm pretty sure they would've blown things out of proportion. Better for it to stay between us, what really happened. I was sort of, er, creative with the events. A little obfuscation, a little fabrication, a little truth sprinkled in.

... Well, if you ask me, the girl has the right to know the truth, I don't care what they would think about that. Especially with all she did to lay rest to her great-granny, I'm not going to punish her with gaslighting.

... Yeah, I'm sure. She has a great potential for magic, not letting those charlatans mess that up.

... Soon I hope. I need an hour more, two max. ust need to go through it all for a final check to make sure I didn't slip up somewhere and write down something I shouldn't have.

... Love you too! See you home soon!"

Author's Note

Thank you, dear reader, for picking up this book. I hope it was a time well spent and that you enjoyed the stories within. If you have the time and energy, consider leaving a review or a comment wherever people leave book reviews, be it Goodreads, The Storygraph, social media or at retailers. Short or long, it goes a long way in helping these tales find their intended audience, and I'm truly grateful for that.

Instead of working on my upcoming novel—the first few chapters patiently waiting for my return—I wrote a couple of stories, one of which was so dear to me that I wanted to publish it in a book. I'm talking about the short novella ***The Mystery of the Lost "Treasure Hunters of Velebit": Overview of the Material***, my first foray into epistolary form and found footage structure. It was originally written in Croatian and published in the online magazine for speculative fiction, *Morina kutija*, but I came to the conclusion, as I usually do, that I want to share it with a wider audience. That meant translating it into English.

The inspiration behind this story was cited inside the novella—the oral traditions of the people living in Velebit's foothills. This is not the first time I was inspired by these folk tales, in fact. If you've read my scifi eco-horror aquatic novella *It Eats Us From the Inside*, you're already familiar with the tale of the hidden treasure in the lost ninth Roman well. If you didn't read that novella, but want even more of Velebit and the different meanings "treasure" can have to each of us, check out that book. It's a genre mash of fantasy, scifi and folk horror, set in a near-future Karlobag, perfect for fans of Lovecraft, and I've heard readers saying I've ruined seafood for them.

But let's get back to our lost treasure hunters. I'll be honest, the main reason this story exists is because I rewatched *National Treasure* and told Vesna, "Hey, we have so many hidden treasure folk tales, you would think we would also have this type of treasure hunting stories, I really want to read something like this, but set in Croatia." And then, of course, I needed to write it. Except, I love horror, and wanted to try out the found footage format, so instead of a more adventurous comedic fantasy with would-be Velebit treasure hunters, you got dark and unsettling queer folk horror.

All of the motifs used in this novella—fairies, werewolves, snakes, the Turks, treasure—are based in real folk traditions. Everything Silva mentioned in her email is a product of my own research and the paper linked is a real paper, and if you understand Croatian and love folklore, I absolutely recommend this. (Fun fact: there's a tiny difference between the original Croatian and the translation in her email. In Croatian, I never had the need to explain why the Turks are such a common motif in our folk tales or why they're cast in the role of a bad guy. But since this is now published for a wider audience, I wanted to add in a few explanations for those who don't know our history with the Ottoman Empire. This is not even scratching the surface of the deep cultural trauma left from their invasion efforts, as seen in much of our literature and art.)

The second major influence on this story is, of course, the narrative fiction horror podcast *The White Vault*. Before the pure genius of that podcast, I wasn't big on found footage. I was never a fan of it in movies (probably the only found footage movie that I like is *Cannibal Holocaust*), and I never understood the popularity until listening to *The White Vault*. I like how the podcast utilized the found footage structure and it showed me its real potential. This podcast lives in my head rent free (sorry for the use of the old meme) and I believe its influence is pretty obvious in the way I approached the form in my story. If you like found footage, horror, an ensemble cast, an engaging mystery, prehistoric research, and scientists in isolated places, I absolutely recommend this podcast.

I also learned to appreciate epistolary form with some great recent horror books, like *The Twisted Ones* by T Kingfisher. I had so much fun with this type of narration, creating unreliable narrators, and finding ways to tell the story between the lines, both in the story about the lost treasure hunters and *Notes and Reports on the Woman in White Incident.*

I also want to point out an easter egg in the novella, and that would be the joke names for the infamous podcasters Vesna Hani-Kriletić, Igor Morinić, and Tonija Zvončarić—that would be the editor of this book and my partner-in-crime, the aforementioned Vesna, and my friend and colleague Igor Rendić, and of course, me. The three of us co-host the Mora FM podcast (in Croatian), where we constantly talk about writing, publishing (Croatian and foreign), speculative fiction, fandom, and so on, and so forth (and we even got the biggest Croatian speculative fiction award for our work on the podcast!). The fake surnames all have meaning, but I'm going to leave that to you to decipher if you want to.

We created Pinterest board with pics from our 2023 research hike, so if you want to check out the hiking trail and the Turkish Door pass, you can check out Shtriga Books' Pinterest for *The Lost Treasure Hunters*. I plan to revisit the hike so I hope for more photos (and a better quality!).

Moving on to the rest of the stories, ***What Lies Tangled in the River Grass*** is a reprint. This short story about a she-wolf and water spirit/fairy from the Croatian folk tales was originally published in the anthology *Folk Tales from the Hinterland*, by Gurt Dog Press. Unfortunately, Gurt Dog Press closed down, and I got the rights back. Since this book already has werewolves and the fae, I felt that the different versions of wolf shifter and fairy from those based on Velebit's stories would find the right place in this book. Rastoke is also a beautiful village and I absolutely recommend you check it out. I only visited it once, when I was on a research trip for my urban fantasy novella; stopped there by accident, fell in love with the mills and the fairy tale atmosphere, and was instantly inspired. I have a friend who hails from there and I hope she won't be disappointed with the story (N., if you're reading this, I wrote this story before the pay bridge, otherwise that would surely be mentioned. :D)

To Stop the Screaming is a result of a vivid nightmare in which I cooked a baby. I don't have a child (only the best dog and the most majestic cat), it was literally a baby I was baking in my dream like a chicken, for some reason. It was so lifelike that when I woke up I could still see the images, seared into my mind. Naturally, I decided it would make for a great horror story. The rest of the story all came around that dream. There's also plenty of real horrors in this story, including religious trauma (yes, I grew up in a traditional Catholic household—the local archbishop mentioned once how my family is a pillar of true Church values—and I went to Catholic high school), rape culture, and the horrible fact of the high refusal rates of abortions in Croatia because of conscientious objection, forcing women to seek help in Slovenia (something that's not financially possible to everyone). Right now, while I'm writing this author's note, we're in the midst of the campaign *My Voice, My Choice*, fighting for abortion rights in the European Union. Croatia is unfortunately seeing a lot of far right campaigning and a rise of far right politicians trying to get abortion completely banned. I'm honestly worried where it will get us and it all sort of spilled over to my darker thoughts, and in turn, on these pages.

Moving from the real horrors to the fictional, Kuma is directly inspired by the blond seductress from *The Blood on Satan's Claw* (1971 folk horror movie). This movie is so ridiculous, and has a certain type of charm, but the cult leader, her white dress and wreath, stayed with me and shaped Kuma. While Vesna was reading this story, she said to me the cult has a seventies feel to it, so I guess the influence is visible. And regarding the whole snake-woman thing, I believe Croatian readers could recognize in this story a sort-of inversion to the very famous children's fairy tale with a snake daughter-in-law, a poor old mother, and her gullible son.

Snakes and snake-women are also common folk elements, and here it felt natural to include them, especially with the more Biblical connotations. I also once read somewhere on the Internet that snakes were of religious importance to the Illyrians, but to be honest, I know very little of that part of our history.

Notes and Reports on the Woman in White Incident is a prequel to my urban fantasy novel *From the Cradle to the Grave*, english translation by Igor Rendić, out in November 2024. After publishing that book, I said I was done with the Dorm and Nana, but it turns out, I was lying. After recording the podcast episode on epistolary form, I wanted to write something in the style of the interviews and notes I have to note in my professional documentation, and that resulted in this story. The only thing missing is the student files, but that would turn this novelette into a novella, and I didn't have any wish to do that.

If you're interested in continuing on with this universe and characters, you can also check out the short horror story of Nana and her wife's meet-gross (opposite of meet-cute), Of Monsters and Dogs, free to read at shtriga.com, and the dark urban fantasy novel with a spoonful of mystery and a pinch of horror *From the Cradle to the Grave* (I'm bad at marketing because I always forget is it a spoonful of mystery or spoonful of horror, and I'm pretty sure I used that interchangeably. The fact is, the book is a combination of urban fantasy, horror and crime mystery, no matter the order.) This universe is a culmination of my interest in Croatian folklore, Slavic mythology, Rijeka's history, and a play with the Croatian dorm system for the teens who don't have the opportunity of high school education in their hometowns, which I recognized was a fun way to have something popular in fantasy (magical boarding schools and such) made local.

I could continue on with the inspiration for everything, but that could end in me writing a whole new book. I love to talk, after all. In the end, I just want to thank all who read the Croatian version of *From the Cradle to the Grave* and got back to me with great reviews, videos, and even a fan mail. Your love for this book means the world to me and gives me the best motivation for writing every time I struggle with mental health. I know this wasn't what you asked when you said you hoped for the sequel, and I'm still not sure if I'm ever going to write a second book and turn this into a series, but I hope you'll like this unplanned additional story, even if it's only a prequel.

Thank you to my talented namesake Antonio Filipović Athan who continuously gives me the best possible art for my covers. You can follow him on IG as @a.th.a.n (he promised us he'll be more active there!) or check out his ArtStation (antonio-athan).

As always, big thanks to Vesna for all the work she does editing my stories even when it's too gross, too disturbing, too graphic. I trust you above anyone else and I'm happy we get to do this publishing thing together.

If you're able to visit Croatia, Northern Velebit is full of beautiful nature and trails, but leave your flip flops at home, have plenty of water with you, and a good pair of sturdy shoes.

About Antonija

Antonija Mežnarić is a Croatian writer, editor, and podcaster who lives and breathes speculative fiction. She writes queer horror and fantasy, mostly inspired by South Slavic folklore. With Vesna Kurilić, she founded the small publishing house Shtriga, which won the ESFS award in 2021 for Best Publisher, and is the lead editor of *Morina kutija*, the online magazine for speculative fiction with a focus on bringing stories by local authors to the wider audience. She's the editor and co-host of the SFERA-award winning Mora FM, a podcast about writing, publishing and speculative fiction, and dabbles in booktube for the Morina kutija channel.

Her passion is promoting speculative fiction, especially queer and feminist books, and Croatian authors, and she can be found at various local conventions discussing different topics at panels and other bookish events.

You can follow her book ramblings on hauntednarratives.com or on Instagram and TikTok @antonijamezni.

Also by Antonija

From the Cradle to the Grave

Secrets, lies, and deadly history come together in this dark urban fantasy novel with a spoonful of mystery and a pinch of horror, inspired by Croatian folk tales.

It Eats Us From the Inside

A quiet, claustrophobic near-future horror novella about changes from the outside and from within, ecological disaster, aquatic dread and Slavic folklore.

Mistress of Geese

A collection of folk horror tales about isolation, loneliness, destructive powers of nature, magic and creatures lurking in the dark.

What Do Nightmares Dream of

A sapphic horror comedy novella about a lonely lesbian teacher fighting against a sleep paralysis demon from Slavic folklore.

About Shtriga

Hidden stories in your pocket.
Scifi, fantasy and horror on the go. Publishing your daily dose of speculative fiction since 2020.
Proud recipient of the ESFS Award for Best Publisher of speculative fiction in Europe, in 2021.

Visit shtriga.com for more information. Follow us on Instagram, TikTok and Facebook @shtrigabooks.

Other books by Shtriga inspired by Slavic folklore and mythology:

Slavic Supernatural:
An Anthology of Slavic-Inspired Speculative Fiction
edited by: Vesna Kurilić & Antonija Mežnarić

A Town Called River
by Igor Rendić
urban fantasy trilogy

Bye-Bye, Babaroga
by Ivana Geček
horror novella

www.ingramcontent.com/pod-product-compliance
Lightning Source LLC
LaVergne TN
LVHW010556160826
845677LV00013B/3145

* 9 7 8 9 5 3 8 3 6 0 2 8 2 *